5
TO
1

ALFRED A. KNOPF

NEW YORK

a novel

Holly
Bodger

5
TO
1

THIS IS A BORZOI BOOK PUBLISHED BY ALFRED A. KNOPF

Text copyright © 2015 by Holly Bodger
Jacket design and interior illustrations by Jennifer Heuer

Visit us on the Web! randomhouseteens.com

Educators and librarians, for a variety of teaching tools, visit us at RHTeachersLibrarians.com

Library of Congress Cataloging-in-Publication Data
Bodger, Holly.
5 to 1 / Holly Bodger. — First edition.
p. cm.
Summary: "In a dystopian future where gender selection has led to boys outnumbering girls 5 to 1, marriage is arranged based on a series of tests. It's Sudasa's turn to pick a husband through this 'fair' method, but she's not sure she wants to be a part of it." —Provided by publisher
ISBN 978-0-385-39153-5 (trade) — ISBN 978-0-385-39154-2 (lib. bdg.) —
ISBN 978-0-385-39155-9 (ebook)
[1. Novels in verse. 2. Arranged marriage—Fiction. 3. Obedience—Fiction. 4. Women's rights—Fiction. 5. Family life—India—Fiction. 6. India—Fiction. 7. Science fiction.]
I. Title. II. Title: Five to one.
PZ7.5.B63Aaf 2015
[Fic]—dc23
    2014023541

The text of this book is set in 12-point Garamond.

Printed in the United States of America
May 2015
10 9 8 7 6 5 4 3 2 1
First Edition

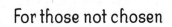

For those not chosen

SUDASA

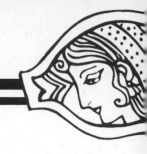

1

One month from today,
I'll wake to a team of
        makeup artists—
        hairstylists—
buzzing outside my door.

At Nani's command, they'll
        swarm.
They'll
        poke
me with their glittery swords,
        paint
me with their honey.

I'll fight the urge to scratch it away,
because I'm
        Sudasa the Obedient
and I must keep my fingers
gluedtogether
like the dolls
Asha and I
left buried under my bed.

When the artists flee,
the designers will inch i n t o place.

They'll
          spin
me in their silks.
          garnish
me with their golds.

They'll lift me onto an easel.
Wait for Nani
to stamp me
DONE!

After that, I'll be placed upon
an elephant—
the only creature who'll appear
more ridiculous than me.

She'll deliver me
to a temple with
          no god.
Then Nani will send me
down the aisle with
          <u>strict</u>
          <u>instructions</u>
          <u>to keep my</u>
          <u>gaze</u>
          <u>off my</u>
          <u>beaded shoes.</u>

The people of Koyanagar will
watch me.

Question me.
                    Love me?
Hate me.

Hate me for not marrying
            their son.
For not bearing
            his ~~children~~ daughters.
For not guaranteeing
            his future.

At the end of the aisle,
            a boy—
squeezed into a black sherwani—
will sit on a chair,
his spine as rigid as its spindles.

He won't look at me;
      won't dare.

I won't look at him, either.
Will look at the woman
in front of him.
The one with the stole of
red.
            The color of love?
No.
            The color of blood.
Blood of birth. Blood of death.

5

The only things that matter
in Koyanagar.

When I stop in front of the woman—
Koyanagar's only marriage officiant—
she'll scan the papers in her hand.
Commence the same speech
she must utter for the
                    two hundred girls
who turn seventeen this year.

Her first words today—
they won't be for Papa.
He doesn't have a say. Can't give me away.
How could he?
You can only give away
that
which is yours to lose.

No. Instead, she'll tell me to
↓ sit ↓
and then motion
for the flowers to come.

Long garlands of lilies.
                    Orange lilies.
The flower of purity.
(Or, some say, pride.)

She'll ignite the fire
of butter and wool.

Tell the boy and me to
        stand.
        link our hands.

She'll tell us to take
                seven steps. Accept
            seven blessings. Spend
        seven seconds
circling around the fire.

When we're done,
she'll present us to the audience.
Me
and my husband:
the boy.

Only she won't call him that.
She'll call him a name.
A name I will not know.
Until then, he'll be a
        n#mber
from the Koyanagar Registry.
Not a boy named
        Ravi.
        Jamal.
        Shahid.
Not a fiancé.
Or a friend.

A n#mber.

Today,
before any of this can happen,
I have to get out of bed.
Have to put on my sari.
Have to open my door.
Have to accept Nani's advice.
Have to pretend Mummy gives some, too.
Have to get in our carriage.
Have to ride through the crowds.
Have to sit in the theater.
Have to wait for my turn.
Have to follow the rules.
Have to smile like I agree.
Have to
Have to
Have to
Have to
        Choose him.

2

I'm a puppet
strung up in a box
hanging over a theater
        of heads.
        of faceless people.

The light in my box—
a dimmed chandelier—
ensures no one will see me
until it's time for my scene.

Until then, I fade into a
gilded armchair with
Mummy and Nani
confining me
like *lopsided* bookends.
        A mouse to my right.
        A rhinoceros to my left.

From behind me, Surina groans
as if she's been forced
to sit on pins.
Her problem is not the
second-class chair. It's that
she has always played

Older Sister.
Poster Girl.
Know-It-All.
And not
  Understudy.

Before we left the penthouse this morning,
I told her to stay home.
Said I'd bring Asha in her place.
At least then I'd have
  help.
  support.
  friendship.
(Best friendship.)

But Nani had
snipped away my suggestion
like a lotus with a wilted bloom.
"The box has only five seats
and your sister must attend.
If you want to bring that Asha girl,
tell your father not to come.
It's not like he *can help you."*

Nani doesn't see
the difference between
what Papa
  can
do and what he's
  allowed
to do.

The men played a game.
Put on a show. Won
            a contest.
            a wife.
            a life.
Life sentence, if you ask me.

Well, I see the difference and
so I flash a smile over my shoulder.
Show Papa I'm happy
he came.

Nani is not so pleased
with her ghar jamai:
her ever-present
son-in-law.
She hisses, *"Sudasa, turn around."*

And so I do.
I face forward, with glassy eyes.
See blurs of orange, yellow, and green
as two thousand people
cram
into rows of fold-down seats.

Once rosy and plush,
twelve years of Tests
has turned them
      tired.
      tattered.
      torn.

These people have been here before.
Those over> thirty as audience.
Those under< as players.
      (Women in my place.
      Men on the stage.)

3

They
       dim the lights.
I
       dim my eyes.
I imagine a time when this stage was used
for *real* shows:
       Dattani.
       Bhāsa.
       Kālidāsa.
A time when this entire theater
was drenched in
       music.
       laughter.
       song.

Not anymore.
No time for plays.
No need for plays.

We have the Tests
to fill the women's cups
with entertainment.
We have the wall
to heap their plates

with victory.
With revenge.

A spotlight illuminates. All
eyes follow it to the   right
of the stage.
All but mine.

I don't need
        to watch,
        to listen,
        to know
what's coming.
Nani already warned me this would be
"a very auspicious moment"
for the eight girls here today.

Our president attends only
a handful of the twenty-five
annual Tests.
The others get a recording
of her never-changing speech.

Before this speech can pass her lips,
her words
repeat in my head
like the notes from the first sitar melody
I tried to learn.

They're the notes I've heard
from Nani

these last twelve years.
The ones played
           for Asha
two weeks ago;
           for Surina
two years ago.

I should be thankful. Thankful my sex
guarantees me the life of a bird.
           Food.
           Safety.
           A home?
More like a cage.

I should be thankful that women—
like our president;
like Nani—
were able to
           lead a revolution.
           form a country.
           facilitate change.

And I am thankful.
A bit thankful.
But this change—although it may be
           the reason life is comfortable for a girl like me,
it's also
           the reason I'm in this theater.
           the reason my freedom comes with a $price.tag.
It's
the reason I

                    must wear the gold sari.
                    must march down the aisle.
                    must marry at seventeen.

It's
the reason I
            must wed a stranger.

The reason a stranger must
            compete
to marry me. Risk
            death
to marry me.

For that, I'm not thankful.

CONTESTANT FIVE

4

Appa didn't try to stop the guards when they came for me yesterday. He didn't kick up a fuss like some of the parents do, crying and begging for more time. He didn't offer a bribe—one the guards would have slipped into their pockets before they proceeded to drag me to the cart like nothing had happened. No, he simply stood at the door in his threadbare robe, waggling his bony finger as he said, "Remember, boy, the seed grows at the same speed, even in the wind."

The guards frowned at Appa's words as if they thought he was trying to trick them by talking in code. That's not what he was doing. This is simply his way. He speaks using only the best words. He tends only the strongest crops. He has saved everything to give me one shot, and one shot only, at a new life.

This advice about the seed—this was him reminding me to be patient because he knows I'm not good at patience. Not normally. But today, with these tests—I've been waiting for the State to select my name from the registry since the day I turned fifteen, and I'd been waiting to turn fifteen since Amma took me aside and told me that our new nation had declared me, and almost all other boys, worthless. That's a whole lifetime of waiting. I can certainly handle another three days.

The other boys in my group clearly got different advice. When they brought us to the theater this morning, the guard pointed at a jumble of chairs marked with a *Group #8* sign and said, "You got a while. Get changed and try to relax." And yet, the pretty boy pulled on his navy kurta and then immediately started pacing like a lion trapped in a two-foot cage. The crippled boy slumped down, putting his head on his hands as if he needed to force it to stay still. The tall boy carefully exchanged his wet shirt for a fresh one and then proceeded to drench it with sweat. As for the young boy—he started sobbing the moment he walked in the back door. Sitting down made him upgrade to loud, shuddering moans. Poor kid. He has probably just turned fifteen and is still in shock that his name was chosen so soon. I suppose I should be grateful that Chance gave me until two weeks before my eighteenth birthday before I was picked. Otherwise, I would have had to leave Appa sooner. Before I was big and strong. Before Appa's plan was perfect. Before I was sure it was the right choice for me.

For now, my only choice is to change into the red kurta the guards tossed at my feet and then sit in the chair they left for me. It's not bad. I have a perfect view of the stage. The woman standing in the middle introduces herself as the director of today's tests. She says we're in for a great honor, and the audience erupts with bubbles of whispers. When she adds, "And here she is, the president of Koyanagar," the bubbles are popped by gasps and claps. I'm pretty shocked as well. I've heard the president on the State-assigned radio many times, but I never even imagined she'd actually be here—in person. There must be someone important at the tests today.

The president is not at all like the powerful icon I imagined her to be. She's more like I remember Amma: small and delicate, with a sari that dances behind her as she walks. Of course, the president is clad in white, the color that shows eternal mourning of a lost child, while Amma never wore white. She wore reds and oranges and deep greens. Colors of celebration and happiness. Perhaps she wears white now. Now that I am dead to her.

The audience goes silent when the president lifts her hand, as if she's about to speak words they haven't heard before. They have. We *all* have. The tests are open to the public, and for those who can't attend (because they have to actually *work* if they don't want to starve), they're broadcast on the only radio station in Koyanagar. When I was about to turn fifteen, I got up extra early so I could finish my chores and then listen to every minute of the tests. But after a few months, they all sounded the same. Different girl, different boys, but the rest: same same same. And still, the people here today have swarmed like flies to a rotting corpse. Someone should tell them they're a bit early. The corpses come *after* the tests.

Standing behind a wooden podium, the president begins the same monologue used every second Monday, when they start a new round of tests. "Fifty-four years ago, at the dawn of the new millennium, my country was a burlap sack bursting at its seams. It had two percent of the world's land but seventeen percent of its people. Our water was poison, and more than half of our people were starving in the garbage-filled slums. A new prime minister was elected who promised to fix everything. He told his citizens they must limit their families to one child. He said he would fine anyone who didn't obey and jail anyone who didn't pay the fines. His citizens obeyed, but not in the way he expected. The citizens didn't want *any* one child. They wanted a child who could help support the family, especially when the elders were too weak to do so themselves. They wanted a child who could carry the family name, inherit the family land. They wanted a child who could attend their funeral pyres and release their souls to heaven. They didn't want a child whose dowry would empty their safes to fill the pockets of another. They wanted a *male* child.

"The people took their money and spent it on illegal ultrasounds. If they didn't hear the words 'It's a boy,' they spent more money on doctors who could quietly make the problem go away. If they couldn't afford these luxuries, they waited nine months and then took care of things themselves. Some abandoned their baby girls in a park, knowing they would be sold to lands far away. Others used a towel. A pail. And a grave."

The president takes a sharp breath and then reaches for a glass of ice water. This pause is partially for effect. She's had one all right. The audience is completely silent, aside from the occasional sniffle or blowing of a nose. This is exactly what she wants. She wants the people to picture these unmarked graves filled with baby after baby after baby so they will long for what comes next. Appa says this is like putting hay in the goat's mouth and then praising it for deciding to chew.

"Three decades later," she continues, "the country found itself with more than six boys for every girl of marriageable age. These boys needed male heirs of their own, but there was only one way to get them. Suddenly a girl—any girl, even a poor, worthless one—could be sold to the highest bidder.

And that's if she was lucky. Some girls were stolen out of their childhood beds. Others were raped, fated for ruin.

"As for the poor boys, they were left without options and full of shame. That shame festered into resentment and anger. That anger spun into violence. That violence left blood. Boys' blood. Sometimes, girls' blood as well. We women of Koyanagar—we'd spent years trying to scrub the blood of our daughters' ghosts from our fingernails. We'd had enough.

"We went to our capitol and told the prime minister that his policies needed to change. He laughed, asking us if we thought we could do a better job running the country. We said we could. He told us to return to our insignificant city— known for nothing but its mangoes and monkeys—and try. So we did. We put our angry boys to work building a wall around our city and its surrounding villages. We abolished the one-child laws, replacing them with those that protected our girls and rewarded their families. We got rid of the innovations that had been used against our sex.

"On 20 December 2041, we posted the eight governing laws of our new nation. We told anyone who didn't like them that they were free to leave Koyanagar as long as it was before the start of the new year. At the stroke of midnight on 31 December 2041, we closed the gates for good.

"As a final reward for the boys who built our wall, we gave them jobs guarding the wall from sea to sea."

She pauses again, this time for a different effect. She wants the audience to imagine these poor boys made happy because they had a purpose. She wants the audience to think of their own sons, or future sons, leaving these tests feeling the same. Not cheated out of a future. Privileged to serve.

She doesn't want to mention that the violence hasn't stopped since the wall went up. The boys are guarding it for a reason: they're supposed to kill anyone who tries to get through without permission. They've been promised a full stomach for their success, a noose for their failure.

The sheltered girls, who never actually see the wall, believe this ruse. They think the guards assigned there are these noble warriors willing to die for them, but they're not. They're still just as angry and resentful, and still just as covered in blood. And they're not at the wall because of their loyalty to Koyanagar and its girls. They're there because, like the forty boys who've come to this theater to compete for the eight girls here today, they have no choice. The State provides their food, their shelter, their shackles for life. It's do or die—or, for many, do *and* die.

The president wraps up with the reason we're here today. "After we closed the gates to Koyanagar, we started the Tests so marriage would no longer be a bidding war. The Tests ensure that every girl gets the best mango from the tree and that every boy—rich or poor—has an equal chance to be picked. As a final step to ensure that marriage will always be fair, we invite you, our people, to join us. We open our doors to your eyes. We open our radio station to your ears. But most important of all, we open our desire for a bright future to your hearts.

"And now," she says, stepping aside with a flourish of her sari, "let the first Test begin!"

The audience breaks into excited applause, as if it's some kind of honor to be chosen to be here, which it's not since the tests are open to anyone with the time or inclination to attend.

And despite what the president may think, the people who swarm here on a regular basis don't do so in order to ensure that things are fair. Only the naive and blind girls, who believe in the noble warriors, would ever believe that. No, these people are here for the sport, and as with every sport, there are only a few possible outcomes for the boys who step onto the stage.

The first is victory. The winner gets a wife and a secure life and future. He gets a roof that doesn't leak during the rains, clothes that don't smell of sweat or mold, and enough food to fill his belly. If he gives his wife a daughter, he might be rewarded with hot baths every second day and a servant to help him with cleaning and meals. He is the epitome of winning. The happy ending everyone longs for.

The second outcome goes to those boys who lose or are not selected to compete before they turn eighteen but who have sisters and thus money. They are sent to the assignment center, where their families can bribe the officials into finding them the best occupation they can afford. For twenty thousand yira, a teaching position will suddenly open up. Five thousand yira, and the only opening might be sweeping the rice mill. It's not a happy ending for these boys, but it's also not a sad one. Many live long lives working these jobs. They do not get to feel the embrace of a girl or the joy of fatherhood, and they will never make enough money to live on their own. Still, they do not starve, and they get State-assigned uniforms and shelter. If they're really lucky, they might even get to sleep on their employer's kitchen floor and eat the food she discards.

The final outcome is the one awarded to the boys who

are poor, like me. When they lose the tests or turn eighteen without being selected, they are sent to the assignment center, where there's only one option available: joining the angry men at the wall. In the world of sport, they are the losers. In these tests, they lose as well. Lose freedom. Lose choice.

Lose life.

SUDASA

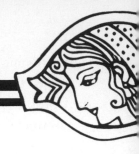

5

Seven hours.
Seven Tests.
Seven girls done
and it's time for me.

As my chandelier becomes a

→ spotlight ←

I clench my bag of rocks.

Mummy puts her hand on top of mine
while Nani squishes her eyelids,
then wakens from her snores
        and
slumber.

We follow the collective gaze
to stage right. To
       my contestants.
       my husband.
Future husband.

The five boys stop in
   center stage,

positioning themselves
against the painted backdrop of jasmine.
A prop.
Like me.

Their identities are concealed
by black masks
as if they're here to dance the chhau
and in the end
I'll be pleasantly surprised
to learn my winner's
a maharaja.

No.
There are no kings here
or anywhere in Koyanagar.

Behind the masks, there are
            boys
and boys are
            strangers
to me.

Until now,
the only one I've been permitted to
            speak to,
            listen to—
            pretend to listen to—
is my cousin.

Sometimes,
if I take my time
returning from the schoolyard after lunch,
I see others:
a sea of blue uniforms
undulating behind thick leaves.

Their voices come in whooshes—
waves—
and I'm always called inside
before their words become clear.

Their moods are clear.
They are the wealthy brothers of girls.
  Happy.
  Well fed.
  Destined to stand on a stage
and perform for a girl like me.

The rest of the boys in Koyanagar—the
  unhappy?
  unfed?—
go to the army school.
A training ground for what
comes after the Tests.
  The jobs.
  The battles.
The deaths.

The director of today's Tests

shuffles the papers on
her mahogany table.

Her white clothes of mourning are
            grayed
in the dim light of the stage.
Her weathered skin is
            lightened
with the powders we women buy
to show we're not deprived.
Not anymore.

She presses her palms together.
Gives Nani a nod.

As one of Koyanagar's founders
and the keeper of its
most precious gem—
            the Registry—
Nani is well known.
By face?
            Maybe.
By name?
            Probably.
By reputation?
            Absolutely.

But this exchange between
the director and Nani—
this isn't polite respect.

There's something about
the nod Nani returns—
the way her focus doesn't
lower with her chin—
it's like she has played this game before.
And while her cards on the table say,
　　　How nice to meet you,
the ones in her hand add,
　　　Once again.

Once again?
I squeeze my eyes tight.
Search for memories of Surina's Tests.

The theater was hot that day,
two years ago.
The rains had not yet come,
but the air was ripe with their promise.

Heat or no heat,
nothing stopped thousands of people
from flocking to see Surina—
the famous face
from the *Love Your Daughters* poster.

She was the reason they wanted
a country like Koyanagar—
a perfect future for a perfect girl—
while I—a second child born
before second children were allowed—
I was the reason they needed one.

I try to focus,
but my memories of Surina's Tests
are like watery milk.

I know Papa sat where he is now,
while I had the chair beside him.
We spent most of the day
taking turns with a
crossword puzzle.

I'd just gotten Shakespeare's Philomel—
Nightingale—
when I heard Mummy say,
"What did you do?"

I tucked away the crossword.
Thought she was scolding
        me.
Or
        Papa?
No. She would never
confiscate
Nani's greatest pleasure.

When I looked up at Mummy—
an apology lingering in my lungs—
I saw her glaring to her right.

At Nani? No.
She was busy looking at the audience.

But Surina—she was staring
straight ahead
with a bit too much effort.

I shrugged it off.
Figured it was simply
Surina
            being
Surina.

Later, in the carriage,
I heard that the rich boy
from the penthouse next to ours—
the one Surina had
pretended not to love
for almost a decade—
had ended up in her Tests.
(And was in first place.)

I thought it was a coincidence.
Just another petal of
good luck
for the girl with the lotus
in her veins.

Is that all it was?

I squish my eyes harder.
Try to remember
            how Mummy looked in the carriage.

Try to remember if she was
      happy?
      surprised?
      upset?
But the director of my Test speaks,
and I must return to my own
reality.

6

The director introduces my cast of contestants
by n#mber:
          One, Two, Three, Four, Five.
I'm not introduced.
Am the blue ribbon they need to win.
The prize of life for one lucky boy.

Disguised as they may be
in their uniforms of equality,
I can already tell them apart.

The first boy wears a navy kurta,
crisp
as a fresh banknote.
His cheeks are pale and smooth.
          He has not seen
a hot day working the market.
          Has not begged
for food.
Or garbage.

He's like my cousin:
a boy born a decade
before three girls.
Once a burden in the old country.

Now an olive—
a luxury few can afford.

In orange and yellow,
Contestants Two and Three stand together.
Their necks as taut
as show horses.
Their bodies
ready
for the whip to strike.

The fourth boy drowns
in a bright green kurta.
His gaze
l
o
w
e
r
e
d
to the stage.
Inexperience
marked on his sleeve.

Next to him, Five
has a red kurta
pulled tight across his chest.
His skin is raw.
His raven hair bluntly shorn
so he will seem like the others.

I've seen poor boys like him before:
        In these Tests.
        On the way past Hun Market.

When Nani leans forward,
I wait for her to repeat
the words she says
when we pass them in our carriage:

"Those tanned boys
with the stained fingers—
those are market boys.
They belong at the wall, Sudasa,
not in your head."

She doesn't say this today.
Instead, she points
at the first boy, in navy.
"That one," she whispers,
her manicured finger
pointing→
so everyone can see,
"that one will give you girls."

The way she says this—
        her words full of confidence;
        her eyes full of the yira signs
that fill our safe when we give birth to a girl—
it's like she knows.
Like she has a crystal ball
for my future.

One she can change with
but
           a
tap.

I examine the first boy again.
           The way his hair
is oiled into curls.
           The hole in his ear
where the black diamond should be.

That's when I know;
           when I'm sure.
He's not like
           my cousin.
He is
           my cousin.

"It's not possible," I start to say,
trying to swallow my shock.
Feeling it get stuck in my throat
like an unchewed grape.

No.
It can't be.

Asha always says I'm more equestrian
than mathematician,
but even I can see
that something
isn't
right.

There were over three thousand boys
eligible
            for the Tests this year.
            for the two hundred girls
turning seventeen.

Eight of the two hundred girls
came here today.
That's eight
for three thousand.
And only one of them
is me.

I could accept
a coincidence once.
Not twice.
And Surina definitely knew
one of the boys in her Tests.

I try to form
            more words,
            more arguments,
            more questions,
but Nani's tongue
strikes
like a viper.

"Anything is possible, Sudasa."
She says this with a grin
playing on her upper lip
and a glance at

~~the director~~ her friend
on the stage.

That's when I know.
    Know Nani
didn't randomly select
my cousin's name
from the Registry.

No. She
chose him
    to perform on this stage.
Handed him
    a leading role in the play called
Me.

7

I want to
        stand. To
        break free from these strings.
              from this box.
              from this life?
I want to
        tell everyone it's a scam.
The Tests aren't fair after all.

I don't.

<u>No one</u> would believe me.
Fair is the first law of Koyanagar.
It's the reason our country exists;
    the foundation of its tower.

And how could I escape?
Where could I go?

In Koyanagar, a girl on her own
would stick out
like a poppy
in a field of mud.

I know. A girl from my school
tried to hide four years ago.

Only her boyfriend
knew where she was and
he refused to reveal
her location.
That was his mistake.
One of his mistakes.
The State didn't need him.
They knew they'd find her
. . . eventually.

They knew she couldn't get
to the other side of the wall—
not without written permission.

It would be no different for me.
And even if it was—
even if I could get through—
I wouldn't survive on the outside.

We're reminded every day:
the people from the old country are
savages.

They would fight for my petals,
ripping them piece by piece
until I'm left but a stem
under their heels.

They see Koyanagar
as the land of peace and plenty. The land
that found the secret to happiness
and then locked it within its own safe.

Their leader wasn't smart like Nani
and her friends. He didn't
      change their laws.
      learn to value their girls.
And now?
They have none left.

      That's why
their people claw at our wall.
      That's why
our noble boys must
             die
trying to stop them.

I glance at my cousin,
      his shoulders
           a w i d e mountain.
      his chin
           the unattainable peak.

It's like he knows he won't become
one of the boys
      at the wall.
      in the jobs.
      on the street.
Like the arrogance he carries is not
      an act.
More like
      a guarantee.

I should have seen it before—
the way Nani

tried to make us two sides
of a sandwich.

Sitar lessons?
"Your cousin should come.
He has an ear for music
and he loves to hear you play."

Riding?
"We must ask your cousin.
He has a way with horses
and he loves the outdoors."

Pottery.
Poetry.
Painting.
        All the same.
        All with my cousin.
        All part of the plan.

The plan that started
when I was born?
Back before Koyanagar?
Back when marriages
were still arranged?

I would have been
the perfect payback
for Nani to give
Mota Masi—her older sister.

After Nani's husband had
crawled into a bottle of McDowell's
and died, Mota Masi
helped get Nani and Mummy
off the street.

She moved them to her new city.
Gave them a place to live.
Introduced them to rich prospects
like Papa.

A marriage between me and my cousin—
Mota Masi's grandson—
would have been a debt marked
PAID
for Nani.

But then Koyanagar was formed,
as were its Tests.
The Tests were supposed to
make marriage
        just.
        equal.
        fair.

The Tests were supposed
to make life better
for the people of Koyanagar.
All but one.

For Nani, the Tests

would have marked her debt
PAST DUE!!!

That is, unless she could
find a way
around the laws she forces others
to uphold.
Find a way to rig my Tests.

No.
No.
No!
I won't allow it.

Although Nani can give my cousin
a place on this stage,
that doesn't
dry the ink on the page.

Even if he has
been well trained—
I

        give the rocks.
I

        pick the winners.
I

        am in charge.

Aren't I?

CONTESTANT FIVE

8

They introduce me as Five and that's who I am, as far as the "honorable girl" is concerned. A number. An option. And not one she'll pick.

They don't tell us her name, and I don't give in to the temptation to follow the audience's stares to the gold-trimmed box with the velvet curtains. I bet she's up there with her family, examining us boys as if we're mangoes laid out on a brass platter, our flesh sliced open for them to dissect. Their glares burn my skin almost as much as the spotlights above the stage. I rub my hand along the back of my neck. The skin is hot and raw. After the guards brought me to the city yesterday, they made me shower with a wire brush and then they cropped my hair with a knife. They said I needed to look like the rest of the boys so "it will be fair." Ha! I'm not sure what difference it makes. These girls don't care how we look. They're here to choose the best slave. Might as well get a dog. Something that knows how to heel and obey.

I step forward, positioning myself behind the fifth podium as instructed. For the next three days, I suppose I *am* a dog. A patient dog. I'll do what they say. Play the game I'm supposed to play. I don't have much choice. I need to make it to the end of the third day—to the final test—and any boy who refuses to participate is immediately sent to the wall. I wouldn't be able to follow Appa's plan if that happened. I wouldn't be able to do anything. The guards at the wall treat radicals like most people treats roaches. Stomp. Squish. Repeat.

I've had the better part of a day to observe the other boys in my group, and a few things are clear. The first is that most of them are scared out of their minds. They don't see this experience as the honor that the director of the tests believes it is. "You have the honor of blah blah blah . . ." That's what she keeps saying, as if the mere act of being invited to fight for one's life is a gift from the gods we're not supposed to believe in anymore. I don't believe in them, but not because religion has been banned since they closed the gates to Koyanagar and said religion was the reason the old country was ripped into rags. I just don't think a being that's good and fair would let a place like Koyanagar exist. Fair means not treating eighty percent of your population like it's worthless. Fair means not making those same worthless people pay for mistakes that were made before they were born. Fair means not giving god-like powers to a spoiled girl in a velvet box while five boys sweat on a wooden stage, wishing—*hoping*—that they'll still be alive next week. Yes, Koyanagar is a lot of things, and fair is not one of them.

The next thing that's clear is that the audience is getting bored. Nothing unusual happened in the seven tests before mine, and some people in the audience have actually fallen asleep. I suppose they expect it to get more exciting at the physical tests tomorrow. That's when the number of competitors usually starts to dwindle. Or perhaps they're hoping to witness a rare dissenter use his first time onstage to voice his refusal to submit to Koyanagar's oppression. That hasn't happened in four years, but it would happen today, with me, if I didn't have Appa's plan. I'd tell the leaders where they can stick their tests and then I'd tell the audience that they don't have to obey because the State tells them to. The people of Koyanagar outnumber the leaders seven thousand to one. They could storm the State Council. Demand a change. Refuse to leave until they got one. That would be me if I stayed— standing at the front of the crowd with my hand raised in a fist. I would demand that the State give the people back control of the coal, water, and electricity. The State holds these things over our heads, forcing us to obey their laws so they won't cut them off.

But no, Appa's plan is better. Appa's plan gives me the chance to search for Amma. Most of all, Appa's plan allows me to live.

The final thing I've figured out today is that the boy in blue is here for one thing, and that's to win. He stopped pacing hours ago, but only so he could jiggle his leg or crack his knuckles over and over again. I don't think he's nervous. Every time the guards have come by to check on us, he has flashed the kind of cocky smirk you only see on a boy with many sisters. He has probably trained for these tests his whole life. What else did he have to do? He didn't have mouths to feed or a farm to tend, that's for sure. And I bet his milky skin has never been exposed to eighteen hours in a Hun Market stall. No, that boy was born to marry a girl like her, and as far as I'm concerned, he can have her.

The director of the tests holds up her palm. "Our first Test for the eighth set of boys was dug up from history."

From the way the audience comes alive, you'd think she'd

unearthed a corpse. She doesn't mean a corpse. She means television. Like the other electronics that once connected Koyanagar's citizens to the rest of the supposedly broken world, televisions were banned after the gates were closed. I know all about them, though. When we're working the land, Appa tells me stories about his childhood. He feels bad that I didn't get much of one and thinks this is better than naught. He has told me—several times—about how he used to sneak into the city to watch the cricket games. His family was too poor for electronics—or even electricity—but he said there were shops that sold televisions, and on the days of the big matches, they'd turn them to face the street so the poor could watch. He said he would wake up at three in the morning so he could be one of the first people on the street and then would stand there for the entire day in the hot sun, without food or water or the chance to pee, all so he didn't lose his spot. He wanted to be close so he could see his favorite player, *the Mighty Bala*. To Appa, seeing *the Mighty Bala* on television was like seeing a fresh spring in the Thar Desert. Appa said he would press his palm against the hot glass, knowing he couldn't touch his idol and yet wishing he could all the same.

Appa continued to go to the city every day until the match was over, sometimes for three days or more. When he returned to Mannipudi, everyone would gather around him while he told them how he'd watched *the Mighty Bala* score ninety runs or, perhaps, even a first-class century. They'd hang on his every word as if he'd touched greatness, and Appa said he felt like perhaps he had.

The Mighty Bala was a legend in our village, and not just because of Appa's stories. He'd been born there—almost a decade before Appa—but when he made it big in cricket, he moved to a fancy condo in the city. His amma refused to leave her home, so he bought her nice things like gold bangles and emerald rings. He was the son every mother prayed for. And he was more than a cricket player. He took a break from the game so he could go to university in England, and when he came back, he married a beautiful woman, which, with the ratio of boys to girls as it was, was as great a feat as any. He was an idol to the people of Mannipudi. A true example of what hard work could achieve. I sometimes wonder if he's the reason Appa came up with the plan. *The Mighty Bala* was the dream Appa had for me, and Koyanagar is the last place I will get it.

According to the president, the years of Appa's childhood were a time of great misery. Appa should have been the most miserable of all since he was as poor as they came. But he wasn't. Appa says, *happiness is like fruit on the vine: yours if you choose.* His family chose to be happy despite their circumstances. They had nothing except a farm and three kids to feed, and they knew they would have lost everything if the authorities had found his sisters hiding in the barn on one of their routine checks. They didn't care. Obeying broken laws was never an option. This was the part the president left out of her speech this morning. She said that everyone in the old country got rid of their baby girls, but this is a lie. The rich could afford to pay the steep fines, and the poor weren't afraid to hide their daughters in places the officials didn't want to look. The president doesn't want to remind people of this. She wants them to believe that obedience is the only option. As is the case with all leaders, her reign depends on it.

I turn to my left as the director goes over the rules of this test. "More honor to have same same same." The young boy is paying more attention to the crowd than to her words. He's probably searching for his family. In the seven tests before mine, I saw some of the boys smile or wave at members of the audience. I bet it made them feel better to have some support. It would be nice, and I know Appa wanted to come. I didn't let him. Didn't see the point. With me gone, he has twice the work to tend the farm and mind the market stall. If he stopped both for three days, it would take him six more to catch up, and that's if he didn't get one of his stomach bouts. All so he could squeeze into a theater with a bunch of bloodthirsty strangers and watch me squirm on the stage. No, it's best this way. We already said our goodbyes before the guards came yesterday, and nothing—and no one—will change what I have to do.

SUDASA

9

Five boys.
Five buzzers.
      Twenty questions.
One winner.

The first ten questions are simple.
They're a chance for my boys
to show they can
      master the buzzers.
      think on their feet.

In truth, I think they're a chance
to show they can take
the truths that have been
shoved

d
o
w
n
↓
their
throats
and regurgitate them
on command.

I listen.
Am supposed to judge.
But that's only an expression.
For this part,
the answers are clear.

The director reads the first question.
Politics.
No surprise.
It was the same for the girls before me.
Will be the same
for the ones that follow.

"Question number one:
Why does Koyanagar need a wall?"
She asks this as if it's a mystery.
Something we don't all know.
But knowing the reason
and stating it in the correct way are
not
the same thing.

A high-pitched buzz sounds
from my cousin's podium.
"To protect its most precious commodities,"
he says,
and with his eyes lifted toward my box,
he adds, *"Its girls."*

Although his words put me on a
pedestal

his eyes make me
the stool he'd use
to ascend there himself.

I am a means
to his ends.
Someone to provide him with
          a penthouse flat.
          silk kurtas.
          hair oils.

Lucky me.

Nine more questions follow.
All politics.
All answers but one
by my cousin.

The director takes a sip of tea,
flipping to another sheet
like she's reading the
pale pink pages of
the *Koyanagar News*
(which everyone knows
contains nothing of the sort).

"Question number eleven," she says,
not looking up from the page.
"Your wife is hungry.
Do you serve her cheese
or a banana?"

My cousin transforms into a
C A R D B O A R D
cutout,
his thoughts as empty
as his understanding
of the word "serve."

The young boy buzzes in,
but when he opens his mouth,
it fills with
a i r.

Time ticks.
The air **thickens.**
His words
do not.

Nani glares at her watch
as if the delay
is a fault in its man-made cogs.

Papa shifts in the chair behind me.
I can feel his tension.
Can feel the way he itches
         to stand.
         to help.
         to yell, *It's a trap!*

The director looks up.
She leans forward.

Reaches for an answer
not yet spoken.

The entire theater goes silent.
At least it does until Five
coughs into his fist.
That's when the young boy
turns his head,
pausing,
his mouth still open.

My cousin presses his buzzer
three times.
> *Buzz. Buzz. Buzz.*
> *Look at me. Look at me. Look at me.*

The director holds her palm
up to my cousin.
"Do you have an answer?"
she asks the young boy.

He turns to her.
"N-neither," he says.
"I m-mean. Whichever
sh-she wants."

The audience unites
in an exhale.
My lungs deflate, too.
No boy who values his neck

would dare feed a banana
to a girl older than seventeen.

Bananas were the food
believed to produce baby boys
in the old country.
Everyone knows that.
Don't they?

As for cheese, we all know
it's supposed to produce girls.
We also know we should
never
admit this.
We'll eat it all right.
Eat it in droves. But we'll say
        it's a craving.
(A craving to have yira in our safes.)

The director returns her focus
to her page of questions
about food. About
what to feed me
so I produce a healthy ~~baby~~ girl.

My cousin's face grows red
as he struggles to find
answers
to questions he can't understand.
(Or maybe, questions ~~he~~ Nani didn't prepare for.)

The second boy struggles with his buzzer,
his left hand smacking it
like it's a toy
that won't move.

I clench the bag of rocks
in my hand. Resist the urge
            to stand up.
            to help him.
            to take the steps Papa would,
if he could.

I focus on the third boy instead.
He has mastered the buzzer.
Is keen to play the game,
but lacks the answers to win.

Only the young boy has those
and he acquires them only
            after
he turns to Five
            first.

Four questions later,
my cousin rouses
the director with a
SLAM
of his buzzer.
"He's cheating!" he yells.
"Contestant Five's
telling him the answers."

The director turns to Five.
She almost looks
        annoyed?
that she has to pay attention
to her mundane routine.

"Is this true?" she says
over her half-moon glasses.

When he gives a polite nod,
I wonder if
he misunderstood the question.
But he adds a smile and
says, *"There are no rules*
that say I cannot."

My cousin argues,
"There are, so!
We're not allowed
to get help from anyone."

Five shakes his head.
"I think you'll find the words are clear.
We cannot get help from the audience.
From each other, it does not say."

Mummy gasps. Papa laughs.
I suck in my lips,
trapping a smile
in my cheeks
like a firefly in a jar.

Shattering
into a million
T I N Y
L I T T L E
p i e c e s.
Leaving him unchanged.

Taking another sip of her tea,
the director flips
to the last
sheet of questions—
the five questions that will decide
if my cousin's
nine-point lead
is enough
to secure a win.

For these,
I cannot hide in the shadows.
I
            am judge.
I
            am jury.
I
            must write down my answer
to each question,
then present my verdict
after each guess.

"Question number sixteen:
Who would the honorable girl

Five's words remind me
of the ones I use
whenever I question
the rules of our household.

Rules about
        who I can talk to.
        where I can go.
        what I can do.
What Papa can do.

Nani says I'm
testing the fence,
whereas Papa—
he always adds a wry little grin
and says it's more like I'm
trying to burn it down.

After flipping through a large rule book,
the director gives her decree.
*"I haven't seen a contestant
try to help another before;
however, Contestant Five is
correct. There are no rules
prohibiting it."*

My cousin's eyes
shoot daggers
across the stage.
They hit Five like
glass on brick.

consider the best artist?"
That's what the director asks.

Not a surprise.
These questions are supposed to be
tailored for each girl,
and Nani is Koyanagar's
largest collector of the old country's art.

Her paintings were gifts.
Thank-yous from the families
who are grateful
for what she has done
for Koyanagar.

In retrospect,
I wonder if
what she has done
has a lot more to do
with their daughters' Tests
than their nation.

I scribble my answer
on the card on my lap.

The young boy buzzes.
"B-B-Bawa?" he says,
his voice cracking
as he stutters out the second syllable.

I shake my head.

What use do I have
for animals?

The third boy buzzes,
wiping his glistening forehead
with the back of his hand
before he says, "R . . . a . . . z . . . a?"
He pauses between each letter
        as if he's not sure
                he wants to say it.
        as if he's not sure
                Raza is even an artist.

He's an artist all right.
Still, I shake my head.
        Too
many   triangles.

My cousin buzzes
and a sneer creeps toward
his mask.
"*Menon*," he says,
his response not a question.
"*I bet she loves the colors.*"

I scrunch up my card with a dull nod.
Wish I only saw gray.

Next question:
"*Who is her favorite poet?*"

I scribble a response.
Know it's written on my face.
Papa started reading me
his beloved Blake
before I could talk.

I was probably the only girl
in Koyanagar
who went to her first day at
the *Koyanagar Girls' Academy*
with "The Tiger"
tucked inside her roti.

I've kept these poems—
these sinews of Papa's heart—
stuffed inside a bear on my bed.

They help me remember
not only who Papa once was
but also who he could be,
if the laws changed again.

The young boy buzzes.
He doesn't look at Five
before he yells,
"T-Tagore!"

He sounds proud
that he can name
a poet at all.

No matter what the school—
assuming they show up—
boys are taught only
useful things.
Things that will help them
            serve
the women in Koyanagar.

It pains me to do it,
but I shake my head.
            Tagore?
No.
            Too much life.
            Too much death.
Too much reality.

My cousin laughs as he buzzes in.
He says *"William Blake"*
like it's the wind.
Something any fool
could sense
with a lick of his finger.

With the spirit of
my beloved Blake,
I nod at my cousin's truth.
Wish I could growl at his intent.

Two more questions of this type.
My cousin right each time.

My blood bubbling
like curry
forgotten on the cooktop.

The final question
from the director:
*"Which does she think better—
riding or cricket?"*

My answer is as obvious
as the nose on my face.
I ride every day.
          Play sports?
Not if I can help it.

But that's not what I write.
My cousin may have won this round,
but that doesn't mean
I can't show him that
he
won't
win
me.

He moves for his buzzer,
but Five beats him to it.
"Cricket," he says,
his voice strong and low.
His eyes

imploring me
to prove him wrong.

Wrong?
          Why would he want to be
wrong?
          Why would he come here with
all the right answers?
          Why would he hand them to the young boy
on a brass tray?
          Keep only the wrong one
for himself?

My cousin interrupts my thoughts
with a laugh.
He knows I couldn't hit a ball
if I tried.
Knows Nani
wouldn't let me
try.

She made Papa give up cricket
when Koyanagar was formed.
It was not a game like these Tests.
No. It was a game he loved.
A game that
          snatched him from Mannipudi.
          paid for him to read literature at Cambridge.
A game that made him
          smart enough,
          famous enough,

      <u>rich</u> enough,
to ~~land~~ buy a wife in the first place.

Even if Nani let me play,
I couldn't do that to Papa.
That would be like the thief
who wears the necklace
in front of the woman
he stole it from.
          Dangling
it in front of her outstretched hand.
          Daring
her to ask for it back.

Before I can respond to Five,
my cousin speaks
without buzzing first.

"Riding," he snaps,
his tone glowering down
from the spotlights above the stage.
"I bet she loves riding."

All turn to me,
Nani smiling
like a cat
with whiskers
drenched in cream.

I shake my head.

Hold up my card.
Flash my untruth.

It's not quite a lie.
She asked which was better,
not which I prefer.
And I might
prefer it . . .
if I played.

Still, Nani gasps,
Papa coughs,
and my cousin yells,
"She lies.
She hates cricket!"

His words are Nani's
but they fail to impress her
nevertheless.
She clears her throat
and he gets
            a glare—and
            a warning
from the director.

"You will not insult
a woman
ever.
Do it again
and you'll get assigned
to the wall."

My cousin drops his gaze,
his nostrils flaring like a bull's.
But angry or not,
this round
is his.

10

I'm brought to the stage.
a golden statue,
paraded
in front of hungry hands.

I keep my own
wrapped around
the bag of rocks
I must give as rewards.

Five for first place.
        Two for second.
                One for third.

They're supposed to symbolize
the winner's ability
to build a wall of his own.
A wall around
        his guarantee.
        his life.
I mean, wife.

As I take the first rock
in my hand—
its surface sandpaper

on the smooth skin of my palm—
what I see is not
            the symbol
but
            the reality.

The stones of Law
that bring us to this trial,
that may order
            sacrifice—
            death?—
for four boys on this stage.

When I place the rock
on the podium
next to Five's rough hands,
I want to cloak it in
an apology.

It's cruel—
the way I'm giving him
            a piece of his future.
            a crystal ball of his own.

I lift my gaze. Try to see
beyond the mask,
into the abyss that are his eyes.
Try to tell him
            I'm sorry
with my silence.

He turns away
  as if he doesn't hear me.
  as if he doesn't want to.
  as if he doesn't care?

No.
He must.
I am his lifeline. His ladder. His only chance.
I may not want him
but he <u>must</u> want me.
Mustn't he?

The director clears her throat,
so I move on,
giving two rocks
to the young boy.

He smiles,
  his soft face marked with a dimple.
  his pride as bright as his kurta.
  his innocence equally as green.

I pass the third boy next.
He's as eager as
a newborn goat,
keen to prove himself. Too
keen to see that
he won't need to walk
in the slaughterhouse.

I stop at the second boy with a
jerk!
Can't not notice
the way his right shoulder
tilts
toward the floor.
The way his right hand lies
limp
by his side.
Like a glove that's
          deflated?
          discarded?

He made it through today—
the intellectual part of the Tests—
but what will happen tomorrow
during the physical?
Or Wednesday
during the practical?
Will he be
          deflated?
          discarded?
too?

I move on to my cousin,
the five rocks
          weighing down my hand.
Their future
          suffocating my hope.

I wish I could keep them.
Wish I could turn around.
Go back home.
Go somewhere else?

I can't.
These may be my Tests
but I'm not really in charge.
Am I?

I place the rocks on the podium.
When my cousin reaches for them,
he
        runs his fingertips
over my thumb.
          Crosses the line.

I snap back my hand.
See him grin like a wolf.
Suddenly feel
like covering my wool.

I know at the moment
one thing for sure:
there's no question
these Tests aren't fair.

Also no question
he knows it.

11

On the way home,
I get the usual silence from Papa.
Not because he has no words.
      (Papa has a PhD in words.)
But here, in Koyanagar, he has
      no right
to use them.
Not in front of Nani.

At least he's allowed
to sit with us now that
Surina's husband has been
      relegated
to the spot by the coachman.

Sliding closer to me,
Mummy squeezes my hand.
Her words come out with the strength
of a puff of rice.
"I know that was hard, beti,
and I wish—
Well—
I think you handled it
the best you could."

Nani hisses,
gripping my other arm
tight.
"She did not!
She will not do that again."

"Do what?" I say,
pulling my arm from her claws.
Ignoring the way Surina
glares at my gall.

"Lie," Nani snaps,
the word as revolting to her
as a cotton-blend sari.
"Embarrass my family."

"Do you mean my cousin?"
I speak with a clearly directed stare.
A stare she avoids
as she turns to the view
of nothing.

"What cousin?" she says,
her tone a fluffy kitten.
"Your mother is my only
surviving child."

I would normally retreat.
Accept her lies.
But this time,

I don't.
I become Blake's tiger as I roar back.

"Cousin. Second cousin.
Same thing.
I know that's Mota Masi's grandson.
And I know he didn't get there
by coincidence.
You can
            force me
to do these Tests.
You can even
            force me
                        to marry the winner.
But I will never pick the one you want.
Never."

Nani laughs
as if my decree is one of the
knock-knock jokes
Asha and I used to tell everyone
who'd listen.

Papa always laughed at them,
even if
            they weren't funny. Or if
            he'd heard them ten times before.
Mummy laughed, too.
(If Nani wasn't listening.)

If she was, Mummy said nothing.
She simply melted in the corner
while Nani crossed her arms
and gave us the same
I'm-not-impressed
glare
that she's giving me right now.

She fingers the two blank charms
on her bracelet and
stops on the one with
Mummy's name.

"I said Never once
but then my husband died
and my daughter was starving—"

She shakes her head.
"The only thing Never will get you
is a stain on your face.
You want to pick a tanned boy?
End up like your didi?

"Tell her, Surina,"
she says, motioning to the front of the carriage.
"Tell her what it's like
to be married to a market boy.
One who's missing half his teeth.
Who can barely hold a fork.
Whose family
begs you

to take food off your table.
Put it on theirs."

I wait for Surina to argue—
to say what she has been saying
since the end of her Tests. Since
the day she stopped being
Nani's favorite. Nani's star.

I wait for Surina to say
that she never loved
          the boy from our floor.
That her husband is her true love.
That she
          loves being married.
          loves having her own wing
          in the penthouse.
That her market boy is now her prince.
That she's happy she picked him;
          happy he's hers.

But she doesn't.
She simply stares at
her charmless bracelet,
presenting an argument equally
as bare.

"See?" Nani continues.
"I told her to choose wisely.
Now she's the one
without a baby girl
in her arms."

Surina drops her hand,
the mask peeling
from her face
like steamed wallpaper.

"Tell her," Nani demands.
"Tell her how you made
that boy from our floor—
the one with the four sisters—
lose in the final Test.
It was your choice and
you picked chess,
        a game of war,
when I told you to choose cards,
           a game of luxury.

"Tell her how you'd promised him
an easy win. How he protested
a little too hard
when he didn't get it.
How he was sent to the wall and
jumped off Agnimar Cliff
instead."

Surina says nothing,
but a tear dissolves on her powdered cheek,
and that—
that tells me everything.

CONTESTANT FIVE

12

When the first test is done, we're shipped off to a squat gray building that has only a few tiny windows along the top. It used to be a medical clinic but is now the place where they keep the forty boys before and after the tests. This is another one of those things that are supposed to make the tests more fair, because if we eat the same and sleep the same and dress the same, then we must be the same, right? Wrong. Appa says *You can't make a zebra by painting stripes on a horse.* He's right. I may look like the other boys to her, but I'm still a farm boy from the coast. I still know how it smells to sleep near the sea, and I still know how it feels to have moist soil stuck under my fingernails. The guards can do what they want to dress me like a clone, but I'll still be me. And I'll still have Appa's plan.

We eat overcooked khichdi at long plastic tables in what probably used to be a waiting room. There's one of those old posters on the wall reminding people to wash their hands so they don't spread germs. Amma once worked as a nurse in a place like this. Before the wall. Before men were banned from working as doctors. Before one of these men—Amma's boss—was told to leave Koyanagar for doing the job his country had paid him to do. Obedience is fickle that way. It's a virtue to its master but a vice to its slaves.

As soon as the guards excuse us, I return to my room. It's basically a cement cell with metal cots stuck to each side. Last night, I had it to myself. Tonight, I'm sharing with the young boy, which is good, because I'd probably punch that boy in blue if I had to spend one more minute listening to him boast about how fresh coriander is supposed to taste and how he cannot possibly sleep without a silk-covered pillow. I don't care that he wants to win the girl and live the life, and I don't care that he obviously knows her and thinks he has it in the bag. That doesn't give him the right to look down on the rest of us because we don't drink sparkling water from crystal goblets. These tests were invented so the rich don't have an advantage. They're supposed to provide an equal playing field for all. They don't, but he could at least pretend like he feels bad about where we come from and, especially, where we're going. He doesn't know if any of the boys in our group have sisters. For all he knows, we'll all be assigned to the wall and that crippled boy will probably die the day he arrives. There's no way he can survive the two months of training. Although it's supposed to make men out of boys, I've heard it produces more corpses than people. Some say there's actually a corpse quota. There's only room for a certain number of men, and if it goes over that, the weakest ones simultaneously decide to jump off Agnimar Cliff. Apparently, their dates of death end up in the Koyanagar registry using the red ink that's rumored to be used for "unnatural causes." Ha! And the State tells us the registry has to be kept secret for "reasons of national security." Sounds to me like the only people they're trying to protect are themselves.

I sit on my cot and take Amma's picture out of my bag. On the night before they closed the gates to Koyanagar, she knelt by my bedroll and told me she had something very important to do. She gave me this picture and said I should keep it in case something ever happened to her. At the time, I thought she meant in the future—the far distant future. I had no idea she'd never return. Obviously, she knew. Appa said she'd wanted us to move to her hometown before the gates closed but he refused to take me away from the only home I'd ever known. I think it's more likely that *he* was the one who didn't want to leave. He's like an old banyan tree: tough and rooted to the soil.

I bet part of his reluctance was due to the same illusion many people had when Koyanagar was formed: they believed the State's promises. They accepted the new regime and all of its laws because they believed things *had* to be better than in the old country. They'd already lived in hell. How could this new country possibly be worse?

I also think that in addition to being stubborn and opti-mistic, Appa didn't believe Amma would actually go without us. Although I was only five when she left, I still remember him rushing to the door every time he heard a noise. He thought she was coming back, and he continued to act like this for days and days. Eventually, he stopped going to the door. Her colorful clothes disappeared from our hut, and the wedding photo of her and Appa moved from the wall to the floor to the bin. Amma became a memory, fading into the distance like a shadow in the setting sun.

It took me years to finally ask Appa why he didn't try to talk her out of leaving. He told me it wasn't an option. He said you can never tie down a person's soul. If he wants to leave, he will, whether he takes his body with him or not. Perhaps that means that my soul will stay here, in Koyanagar, even when I leave. Perhaps this soil is a part of me, like it is with Appa.

I place Amma's picture under my pillow. I've slept with it every night for twelve years. The picture is thin and crinkled, the same way I imagine she would be. Will be? No. I can't allow that to fog my thoughts. I may find her, but I may not. She can't be the reason I go. I must focus on all the horrible things about Koyanagar, like when, four years ago, that boy Vikram was sent to his death because he refused to tell the State where his girlfriend was hiding. Or like the boy we saw last year in an alley behind the market. He was lying against a pile of old crates with lidless eyes and a swollen tongue. Appa figured he'd been dead since the night before. That meant hundreds and hundreds of people had walked by and thought, *He's not my problem.* Not Appa, though. He insisted we take the boy to the sea and give him a proper funeral pyre. I understood why Appa wanted to help free the boy's soul for rebirth, but if it had been up to me, I would have taken his body to the State Council and I would have said to them, "Is this what you meant when you said that you've fixed all the problems of the old country? Because this boy doesn't look fixed to me."

I unclench the pillow in my hand. Next to Amma's picture, I put the single rock I won today—the one the girl gave me because she had no choice. Like me, she has to make it appear like she's following the rules, even if it's obvious to everyone—including her *friend* in blue—that she has already made her decision. I hope she's sitting in her air-conditioned flat, seething because I refused to thank her for that forced look of pity she shot my way. She wants me to bow down and kiss her beaded shoes and beg her to choose me, but I'm not going to give her the satisfaction. I don't need to be her choice, and I don't need her.

I flatten the hard pillow and flip over on my back. I close my eyes and press my palms over them. I try to pretend I'm at home. I try to smell the ginger tea Appa makes every night before bed. I try to hear the tide whooshing against the rocks, but I can't. All I can hear is the lightbulb buzzing from the cement ceiling above me. Last night, I searched for some way to turn it off. When I couldn't find a switch, I stood with one foot on each cot and managed to unscrew it from the socket. I can't do that now. Not with the young boy already under his covers.

I roll over toward the wall and pull the wool blanket up to my forehead. It itches at my neck, so I pull it back down. I cover my eyes with my arm instead. Then I count. Rows of eggplants and soybeans. Pots full of mustard and garlic and chilies. Lines of trees teeming with lemons and limes and mangoes and bright red cherries.

I'm almost asleep when I hear the young boy say, "Thanks. F-for your h-help today, I mean. A-about the cheese. I know wh-what you said about the rule book and . . . and I don't know wh-why you'd help me, but th-thanks anyway."

"It was nothing," I tell him. This is partly a lie. I was supposed to keep my mouth shut for this round. No one would ever wonder why a stupid market boy couldn't answer a bunch of trivia questions. But then the boy in blue started to rattle off all the answers with that satisfied sneer on his face and . . . well, so much for being patient. Sorry, Appa. I'll be better tomorrow. That boy knows I'm watching him now. Hopefully, that'll be enough to make him think twice about bringing his rich-boy attitude to the physical tests.

I return to my counting, and the young boy speaks again. "Sh-she's pretty, d-don't you think?"

He means the girl, and he's right, I suppose. Like with the president, she wasn't what I expected. She was still like the girl from the *Love Your Daughters* posters—adorned in fancy jewels and paint—but her hair was in a plain braid down her back and she didn't prance like she was queen of the place. It was like she was doing what Appa calls *wearing someone else's trousers*. She just didn't seem comfortable. Perhaps it was me who made her feel that way? She would normally be sheltered from someone of my caste and gender. Someone she believes is probably a thief or savage. Plus, she seemed perfectly confident when she got to the boy in blue. But then, he's more of her people. Rich. Beautiful. Spoiled.

I mumble a "Mmmm-hmmm," and the young boy continues, his voice full of energy. "Are you f-from one of the f-farms on the coast? I've never b-been, but they say you c-c-can see clear across the sea on a clear day. Is that tr-true?"

I picture the cerulean sea that I've woken to every day of my life, and part of me wants to tear off a piece of my memories and share it with him like warm roti. Then he would know what it's like to see the white-capped waves breaking on the rocks, and he'd know what it's like to truly believe that another land exists, because you'd seen it with your own eyes. But no. This is not the market, and he's not asking me to spare some bruised fruit. He wants a friend. Someone to tell him he won't lose, and the wall won't be so bad if he does, and if it is, we'll face it together. I can't do that, and not because it would be another lie. Appa says, *The man with cement shoes cannot run.*

I can't afford to care about someone else. Leaving Appa—
the only family I have, the only home I've ever known—was
hard enough. If it weren't for Amma, I don't know if I could
go through with it. Even if it meant a lifetime married to a
spoiled girl or, worse, working in the army. I'd never tell Appa
this, though. This plan is his greatest dream, and I'd sooner
stab my own heart than break his.

I mumble another "Mmmm" and then pull my pillow
over my head.

DAY TWO

SUDASA

13

Day two.
    Two more Tests.
Eight more hours in an
        airless
trophy case.

When Papa was young
and they called him *the Mighty Bala,*
he came to this round arena
to play cricket:
a game that lasted for days.

Now thousands of people
pack in
for a different game.
One that goes for eight hours
but lasts a lifetime.

Today's Tests
are kept secret until we arrive.
That keeps things fair.
Fairish.

The moment I enter my box,
I scan the nearby field.

A two-toned ball on
a mass of green with
two netted goals
inside a painted rectangle.

Football.
I know it well.
Know how to avoid it.
Try to avoid it.

Our teachers at the academy
usually insist we play.
They say we need
moderate exercise to stay healthy.
Translation?
We need moderate exercise
       to get pregnant.
       to serve our only purpose
in Koyanagar.

We're allowed jobs . . .
                 eventually.
Jobs the boys aren't trusted to do.
      Medicine.
      Law.
      Politics.
Teaching other girls?

They'd never give me
a position like that.

They'd be worried I'd be like Papa:
     Full of opinions.
Not like Mummy:
     Full of fear of speaking them.

A loud horn sounds and
all eyes turn to the director
in the center of the field.

She explains the rules of this Test:
1. The forty boys have been randomly
     divided into four teams of ten.
2. Two teams play the first game.
3. The two others play the second.
4. Former pros guard the nets.
5. A single point will be awarded for each goal.
6. Any boy who refuses to play
     will be immediately disqualified from the Tests.

The crowd cheers as the first
two teams take the field.
I scan the rainbow of kurtas.
Find my second and third boys
on the first team.

They wait for the referee
to blow the whistle.
Their
     fear
hidden behind their masks.

Their
     inexperience
marked in the way
they face the wrong direction.

Ten minutes go by,
and my third boy gets a point
from someone else's mistake.

Part of the audience cheers.
The other part boos.
And yet, mistake or no mistake,
a point is better than nothing
and nothing—
that's all
my second boy has.

He doesn't even try.
He just hovers by the goal,
a defender
in a game
where only offense matters.

I find this odd when I consider
the wager
of this war.

Then I zoom in
and the microscope shows that
stakes
are not his problem.

His right leg—
barely more than skin and bones—
arcs outward
as if his knee were a door
ripped off its hinge.

He has no chance
   in this round.
   in these Tests.
   in this life.

14

A whistle signals
the end of the game.
A second whistle,
the start of the next.

My cousin's entrance
provokes
       looks,
       whispers,
       gasps,
and not because he
takes
center field as if it's his kingdom
and everyone else
his lowly pawns.

The reaction is to
his outfit—
the one he wore to play
a sport. Any sport:
       Cricket?
       Badminton?
       Rugby?

And yet, he's wearing
      cleats,
      shin pads,
      striped socks,
as if the sport
was not a secret
at all.
Not to him.

Standing opposite him—
the gentle breeze to his cyclone—
is my young boy.
His kurta fades into the mass of green,
his legs poking out like two
wilting weeds.

I don't see Five
      until the ball is in play.
      until everyone moves.
Everyone except him.

Unlike my young boy,
he doesn't look unfit.
The opposite.
He looks
made
for the field.

He's a sheen of
bay coloring

with black points of hair,
and he reminds me of the
Marwari at my riding club.

All power in pause,
and as gentle as a foal,
but if he wanted to,
he could crush you
like a nut.

I part my lips
        to argue,
            to remind him
he <u>must</u> play.
And yet the fact that he
doesn't
makes me want to say it even
LOUDER!

Am I really that bad?
A prize not worth winning?
A companion less desirable
than the *Grim Reaper* himself?

Maybe
for him.
Too bad not
for everyone else.

15

Two minutes into the game,
my cousin scores his first.
No surprise.
He has prepared for this moment
his whole life.

The other girls don't cheer.
I stay silent, too.
My cousin's goal
        doesn't help them.
It definitely
        doesn't help me.

Nani doesn't agree. She breaks my silence
with a clap and a hoot.
        Her allegiance—
        her direction—
as clear as the sapphire sky.

Three goals later,
my young boy gets the ball.
He goes
        for the goal.
Gets
        my cousin's cleat instead.

He falls to the ground,
clutching his shin.
     Blood seeping
between his fingers.
     Cries pouring
from his lips.

No one on the field goes
     to help him,
     to move him,
     to comfort him,
and I wonder if
they've forgotten compassion.
If the feeling was flushed to the sea
     with freedom.
     with opinion.
With choice.

I look over my shoulder.
See Mummy's eyes
     rimmed in red.
See Papa's jaw
     set in rage.

And so I stand.
Make a stand.
Don't know what else to do.
Can't 'see another's grief
and not seek for kind relief.'

Nani grabs my hand,
her tone a plank
when she commands,
"Sudasa, sit."

I pull away.
Want to ask her
if she'd feel the same
if that were her grandson
moaning in pain.

But sadly, I know the answer.
Nani's allegiance is to her
anger
         and
anger
runs deeper than blood and skin.
It's set in bone
and bone, once broken,
<u>never</u>
heals the same.

The young boy hobbles off.
The game starts again.
But it's not the game
I was watching before.

My strong silent horse
sets his sights on a target—

not the goal.
He's after my cousin.

He hovers behind him.
Steals the ball.
Gets in the way.
Whatever it takes to show my cousin
his moat
is not secure.

My cousin endures,
and yet as time draws near the end,
he starts to lose
> his manners.
> his patience.
> his lead.

The next time Five
tries to take away the ball,
my cousin gives him
an elbow.
Gets a gush of blood
in return.

Five stops in place,
and with a quick swipe
of his nose,
he leaves a mark
much less visible than the
shock
on my cousin's face.

Five turns sculpture again.
Until
        my cousin gets the ball.
Until
        he's almost at the goal.
Until
        it's seconds before the end.

And then, with the power
of a stallion,
and the innocence
of a foal,
Five flattens my cousin
like he's a
leaf
on the ground.

I jump to my feet.
See Nani do it, too.
But her stance is in
        protest,
whereas mine is in
        support.

My cousin stands,
his face a kettle at full steam.
He wants a fight.
Has not the fists.
Goes for a sword of lies instead.

"He tripped me!" he tells the referee
as he clutches a healthy knee.

"And it wasn't by accident.
He did it before.
He should be disqualified."

With a glance at the young boy
doubled over on the bench,
the referee listens.
Nods. Then
points to me:
The real judge?

CONTESTANT FIVE

16

Appa says, "There are no bad people. Only bad choices." I thought this was true before I met the boy in blue, but now I know Appa was wrong. There are definitely bad people, and I'm watching one of them stomp off the field like a spoiled little girl. As he passes the wrinkled old water wallah, he swats away the cup the man is holding, spilling it all over his grayed dhoti. He kicks divots into the grass and spits words that have never passed my lips and never will.

I glance at the girl in her box. She looks almost as angry as him. Her arms are crossed, and her brow is so creased I almost can't see her jeweled bindi. I bet she never expected someone to challenge her precious rich boy. I bet she's standing there seething because I made him look bad and that will make *her* look bad when she picks him.

Good.

If she wants to marry a cheater, she'd better get used to wearing his shame.

She turns in my direction. I hold her gaze long enough to make sure she knows I'm not sorry for what I did. Yes, I should be, but not because of her. Because of Appa. I promised him I would fol- low the plan, and here we are, two tests in, and I've deviated from it twice. I must be more careful next time. The plan won't work if I get disqualified. Or worse, if I win. Ha! As if that could ever happen.

I hear some yelling, so I turn back toward the boy in blue. He's screaming at the audience, pointing at the field and then at me and his slightly soiled sock. Although a lot of people are watching him, I can't tell if any of them care that he's upset. The ref certainly didn't. After he heard the rich boy's same complaints, he told him the girl's in charge of who wins and who loses and then he took off for the change rooms. I can't say I was surprised. His presence here today is part of his State-assigned job, and I'd be willing to bet that caring about us is not part of its description.

I turn back, pretending to scan the audience, although what I really want to know is whether the girl noticed the rich boy's tantrum. Is she angry that the referee didn't kick me out—that he left it to her to do the dirty work? Or was that merely the finale of their show? The audience is dying to see some real competition. Half of them jumped to their feet when I tackled him, and I'm sure I heard some cheers when he elbowed me in the nose. Perhaps she told him to go after the young boy because she knew I'd react. Again. Perhaps they wanted to show everyone that a boy like me might be bigger and stronger, but can never beat a boy like him. Not when it counts. And perhaps they're right. I will finish this test with no rocks. By most people's standards, that's nothing to be proud of.

I allow myself to glance at the girl for just long enough to see that she's talking to the woman with the white hair. Her grandmother, I suppose. The woman's hands are flailing about, making her gold bracelets bounce around her wrists like a tarp that has come loose in the wind. She's obviously angry about something as well. Then again, women of her generation are *always* angry. I wouldn't be here otherwise.

I drop my gaze to my feet for a moment so they won't think I'm watching them. But I'm dying to watch them. I count—

One . . .

Two . . .

Three . . .

Four . . .

—and then I pretend to study two men in the stands right behind her box. The girl isn't nodding like she agrees with her grandmother or bowing like she knows she must act like she does. She actually looks even more annoyed than before.

Strange. Could her grandmother be concerned about having a cheater in her home? Women like her have worked very hard to make sure boys know their place, and that rich boy isn't acting like he knows his. Still, he scored the most goals, and the girl would also be a cheater if she didn't award him the five rocks. Perhaps that's why she's angry? Perhaps her grandmother is telling her she must choose the most respectable boy and she realizes that her precious rich boy is many things, but not that.

I'm about to look away when the grandmother points at me and waggles her finger as if to tell her granddaughter she can't pick me, either. But why would she have to tell the girl that? She doesn't want me.

Does she?

Of course she doesn't. I'm poor and uneducated and would never amount to anything more than a farm boy if I stayed in Koyanagar. How could I possibly be good enough for a stranger when I was not good enough to keep my own amma? Even if she hated Koyanagar and thought the State was corrupt, and even if she had never fallen in love with Appa after their marriage was arranged, she would have put up with these things if she loved me enough. I know I would put up with them as well if Appa asked me. But would Appa do the same for me? He refused to leave Koyanagar when Amma asked him, and he wouldn't agree with me going if it was only to find her. I tried to explain to him once why I wished I could see her, even if it was only for five minutes. I told him I felt like a wheelbarrow with no wheel. He shrugged and said, "Boy, if you've lost your wheel, then you must use a rock instead." He didn't understand why I need to know why Amma did what she did. She left me, a young boy of five years of age, in a country that had decided that boys were dispensable. As far as I'm concerned, I'm like those baby girls Koyanagar's grandmothers had to abandon in deserted parks, only those girls were left because their mothers had no choice, while I was left because my mother *did* have a choice.

And she didn't choose me.

SUDASA

17

The second Test's complete.
The boys all line up.
Eight tidy rows,
though they're not tidy
at all.

Some beaten.
Some bruised.
Some covered in dirt.
Most hurt in some way. Almost all
in pride.

I wait in my place
        while the other girls go.
        while they award their eight rocks
to the remains of their
battalions.

I've four boys left,
with my second one disqualified
for not playing. He's
relegated to the fate
Five wanted for himself?

Of my four who remain,
only two boys scored,

and yet the rules are clear:
I must reward the winners.

Winners?

I run the rocks through my fingers
   as I pace back and forth.
   as I try to distinguish
between
   foul
and
   fair.

If Asha were here,
she wouldn't vacillate.
To her, decision's a chessboard.
To me, it's a blur of muddled gray.

I stop at the third boy
and place a single rock
in his outstretched hand.
He takes it with a smile
and a fervent *"Thank you."*

I turn to the young boy,
his head
   a snapped branch;
his leg
   as broken as
his will
   to go on.

I know that he's done.
He can't continue to compete.
And yet, if he doesn't,
he's disqualified, too.

I could award him
but a smile.
I know he'd understand:
        I have no choice.
        I must follow the rules.

But as I grip the rocks,
tell myself to step away,
I find I can't;
        can't tread a path paved
with his pain.

So I place two rocks in his hand,
and I say, "You played fair,
and to me that's worth more
than a hundred balls in a net."

I steady myself
        as I move on to Five.
        as I wonder if I can crown him
the winner of best intent.

I part my lips to speak.
Nothing comes out.
My words are like Mummy:
butterflies

                    trapped
inside a net.

I meet his eyes instead. They're
dark. Almost black.
They contain
            no praising.
            no pleasing.
            no pleading.
Just nothing.

Is he like me?
Here by force? Here to vie
for a prize
he doesn't want?

But why?
Would he really
            rather fight?
            rather die?
            rather do anything
than win me?

What's wrong with me?

I glance at the seven other girls,
who've returned to their boxes.

I'm not like them,
those vapid, selfish girls.
Those girls who've made

an idol
of Surina—
the *Poster Girl* with the ~~perfect~~ life.

No.
I want
> a future.
> a choice.
> a place other than here.

But here we are,
and award I must,
and if I'm forced to choose
a winner—
at least for now—
I choose him.

I take out the five rocks
so I can place them in his palm,
but he snaps his hand away
as if I offered him fire instead.

"Keep going," he says,
the words soft on his lips.
"Play the game.
Follow the rules."

The rules?

I want to take the rules.
Push them off Agnimar Cliff.

Watch them smash on the rocks.
Watch them sink in the sea.

But he can't share my anger.
He's not shackled by the rules.
They only say
                he must compete.
They don't say
                he must win.

So I obey like a prisoner.
Wrists = bound.
Ankles = in steel.
Freedom = nowhere in sight.

When I give my cousin the five rocks
that bring his total to ten,
the injury he had on display
cracks like ice
in tepid water.

Rules?
No rules?
No matter to him.
What matters is winning.
And not just winning me.

18

A break before the next Test. Time for us
        to reflect—
        to be influenced
(more like lectured . . . again)
by our families.

Nani has little more to say.
She has looked at the starless sky.
Is sure my husband
"will be chosen by dusk."

I want to remind her there are
                three
     more
  Tests.
  Three
     more
            chances
for me to choose another.

But to her, this is neither a game of choice
nor a life of choice.
It's one of influence:
        Hers.

And one of acceptance:
Mine.

She leaves me with Surina instead.
Leaves me to peer into her crystal ball.
See a future
I don't want for myself.

*"It's hard to imagine that Papa
was once a star here,"* Surina says.
"The Able Bala.
That's what they called him."

"Mighty," I correct her.
"They called him Mighty."

I know this.
He has shown me the box of glory
hidden inside his closet.
Tucked away where reality—
and Nani—
can't see.

I know he misses those days. Know
he sneaks off to the market
so he can trade memories
with his former fans.

Surina doesn't know this.
Or doesn't care.
She rolls her eyes

as if it isn't possible that
a man was once
      loved.
      honored.
      celebrated.
As if it isn't possible that
a man could want to be
      loved.
      honored.
      celebrated
once again.

"So why didn't you listen to Nani
and pick cards like she told you to do?"
That's what I ask Surina,
and I don't need to tell her that
I'm talking about her final Test.

She waves my words away
as if I'd offered her more tea.
"Then I'd be a cheater,
and I promised Mummy-ji
I'd be fair."

I want to laugh at the irony.
I'm sure Mummy did, too.
To Surina,
     fair
              is the weather.
     fair

                        is a complexion.
          fair

                        is not
                        something you are;
                        something you do.

"So that's it?" I say as the puzzle
pieces slip into place.
"You were going to pick cards,
but Mummy said she would
<u>never</u>
forgive you if you did?
You picked chess so you could
show her that you
weren't a cheater like Nani?"

Surina shrugs.

"Would it not have been better
          to cheat
for a life of love
          than play fair
and get one of hate?
Because it's true—
this happy-wife thing,
it's all an act?"

Surina examines her manicure.
"Happiness is
          food.
          a home.

clean clothes.
I have all of those."

I slap away her hand.
"You don't believe that.
You were the one
who went on State radio and said
you couldn't wait for your Tests.
You told all of the girls in Koyanagar
that <u>you knew</u> you'd find
love
in yours."

Surina's blue eyes grow clear
as she snaps her response.
"Love won't give you a daughter,
and only a daughter
will keep you alive.

"If you think you're here to find
love,
you've missed the point of these Tests.

"You're here to find a man
to put charms on your wrist
and yira in your safe.
That's the only thing that matters
in Koyanagar."

Her words leave the taste
of bile in my throat.

Has marriage turned
my own sister
into Nani?
Has it made her give up
on happiness?
Would it do the same to me?

No.
I didn't want—
expect?—
love
from these Tests—
from this life?—
but that doesn't mean
I will accept misery instead.

Folding my arms across my chest,
I become a stubborn camel as I say,
"I won't do it," half to myself.

Surina laughs.
"You've been sheltered.
So was I.
A luxurious home.
Private school.
Gifts of gold.
But if your husband's family told you
they'd starve if not for you,
you'd understand why you must
have a daughter."

Her hand moves to her belly
and I wonder
      if I was wrong?
      if the thing that's empty
is a little higher
than her waist?

"Are you pregnant?" I ask her just
      before she turns away.
      before she drops her hand.
Nods her head.
Speaks again.

I open my mouth
      to yell.
      to cheer.
      to congratulate her.
Nani has spoken of nothing
but this for two whole years.

"You cannot tell anyone," Surina says
before I can speak.
"Not until I'm sure it's a girl."

With a furrow of my brow, I say,
"They'll find out if he's not.
You can't hide after
he's born!"

She responds in a tone
so close

to Nani's
it coils a chill around my spine.
"I am the Poster Girl *of Koyanagar.*
I may not have chosen
the ideal husband,
but I will not
make another mistake.
I will not have a baby boy."

"You don't know for sure.
You might—"

She cuts me off,
her words slicing
like the edge of a knife.
"I
Will
Not
Have
A
Baby
Boy."

I open my mouth.
It takes a minute
before her meaning
          slices through my brain;
before words
          slide off my tongue.

"But that's illegal.
Impossible.

People might hope—even try—
to conceive a girl,
but they wouldn't—"
I shake my head.
"It's impossible.
Not even at the market."

Surina smiles.
Not a happy smile. A smile
        of knowledge.
        of power.
        of experience?

"You should listen to Nani-ji.
Anything's possible
if you have money in your safe."

I shake my head.
Say, "Nai. Not that.
That's why Koyanagar exists.
That's why we have the wall
to prevent it."

Surina points to the field
as if the grass
has secrets of its own.
"You saw that disabled boy
competing for you.
Do you think a mother would want
a boy like that in her belly?

"This is the real reason
the ratio will soon
be down to
three to one.

"It's still happening
to the unwanted.
The only difference is
they're no longer girls."

I open my mouth to reply—to ask her
        if she has been pregnant before.
        if she has done *that* before.
But there are no words
big enough
to fill the crater
in my stomach.

Surina leaves me boiling
so she can fill her glass
with more sherbet.

I wait in place.
  Wait to be called to my seat.
      To do as I'm told.
Because I'm *Sudasa the Obedient.*
(More like *Sudasa the Fool.*)

I see Nani
sitting comfortably
with her best friend, Smirk, and

I want to
        stomp.
        pour the pitcher of ice water over her head.

I want to
        show her
        her Frankenstein.
Make her see that everything—
        the Tests,
        the wall,
        the deaths—
everything was supposed to be
worth the price
of keeping history
buried with our ancestors.

But it wasn't.

Instead of fixing things,
        of making changes,
        of making improvements,
all they've done
has been to break them
in reverse.

CONTESTANT FIVE

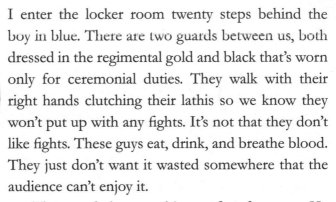

19

I enter the locker room twenty steps behind the boy in blue. There are two guards between us, both dressed in the regimental gold and black that's worn only for ceremonial duties. They walk with their right hands clutching their lathis so we know they won't put up with any fights. It's not that they don't like fights. These guys eat, drink, and breathe blood. They just don't want it wasted somewhere that the audience can't enjoy it.

The guards have nothing to fear from me. He may be the most arrogant, conniving, ruthless boy I've ever met, but that doesn't mean I have a reason to fight him. Not now. He got the five rocks he wanted. I got the none I wanted. It was close, though. For a minute there, when the girl was standing in front of me with her eyes all big and brown and the five rocks in her smooth palm, I was sure she was going to give them to me. Part of me wanted to let her, if only so I could see the look on his face when she did. Bet he wouldn't have waltzed in here with his sneer then! Still, it doesn't make sense that she would even consider giving them to me. Could she be finally realizing he's not what he pretends to be? That he's what Appa calls *a snake resting in the sun*? One that's curled into a ball on a nice, sunny rock, luring you into believing that you can tiptoe by?

I stop at the locker that has *Group #8, Contestant Five* scrawled on a piece of beige tape. When this stadium was used for cricket, these lockers probably had brass nameplates with fancy calligraphy spelling names like *the Mighty Bala.* They probably had leather benches and big televisions and tables full of samosas and sugarcane juice. Not anymore. We boys are like traveling cattle. We're not stopping for long and will soon be replaced by a fresh herd.

On the wall next to my locker is one of the same schedules that are plastered all over the walls and doors of the stadium. They used thick, cream-colored paper and gold calligraphy so the audience will forget that they're spending their Tuesday sweating on a hard bench seat, and so we boys would forget that we're spending it fighting for our lives. The precious girls have nothing to forget. They spent the morning in sheltered boxes while male servants used palm leaves to provide them with a gentle breeze.

I run my finger down the program. It says we have a thirty-minute break before the third test. Really, the officials need time to clear out the injured and disqualified, and by "clear out" I mean ship them off to the assignment center so they can find out how they're spending the rest of their lives, short as they may be. No one actually cares if we get a break, and I can't imagine what the girls need a break from. Occasionally watching us between sips of lime sherbet? Yeah, must be exhausting. That's probably the real reason the wedding is a month after the tests. It's not because they've analyzed the girls' exact times of birth and have decided it's an auspicious date for a marriage. It's because the girls need to

127

recuperate after leaving their air-conditioned homes for three days in a row.

I open my locker and glance in the cracked mirror on the inside of the door. There's a trace of blood above my lip. I don't bother to wipe it away. It's more me than this haircut and these clothes. I squeeze the bridge of my nose. Although my eyes water, I can tell there's no break. I laugh to myself as I imagine what Appa would say if he found out I broke my nose for a fourth time. He was always saying to the men at the market, "My boy, he has a body of brick and a nose of glass." In fact, he said it so many times that some of the men took to asking me if it was going to break if the rains fell too hard. Although it was kind of annoying, I didn't want to ask Appa to stop. I am everything to him. I bet there aren't many boys in this country who could make such a claim.

Ripping my team number off first, I remove my kurta and then turn it over so I can check for bloodstains. There are several drips on the front, but they barely show on the bright red cotton. I wish they'd assigned me yellow. Appa says *an honest man wears his scars on the outside,* and I'm not ashamed of getting bloody, any more than I am of having to work. I would be more ashamed if I came here to cheat, all so I could spend my life letting some girl boss me around.

I glance in the mirror again. The boy in blue is looking in his as well. He's preening the front of his hair as if he's a peacock about to go on display. I bet nothing would make him happier than a life of guaranteed nothing. Sure, he'll get to prance through the market and bark instructions at the coachman. I'm sure she has one—a girl like that. She might even have menservants who cook and clean and shop and respond to everything she demands with "Yes, lady. Anything you want, lady." The only thing her husband will have to do is sire some daughters, and then his life will be done. He'll have no purpose other than as a father, and what purpose is that, really? The women make all the decisions. They wouldn't even need us if they weren't so desperate to produce more girls. It's their own fault this isn't as easy as it used to be. Before the wall went up and it became illegal—really illegal—to interfere with a pregnancy, doctors they deported, like Amma's boss, had machines that could tell if a woman was pregnant with a boy or girl long before the baby was big enough to make the woman's belly swell. If a woman didn't like what the machine found, the doctor took care of it for her.

After Amma's boss lost his medical license, his patients claimed they'd been tricked by him. They thought his machine was taking pictures to make sure their babies were healthy. They said they allowed him to poke at their insides for the same reason and even agreed to take the pills he gave them because they thought the pills would make their babies stronger. This didn't happen. By the end of the day, every single one of his patients said she was visited by the blood.

I was barely five when this happened, but I still remember Amma crying every day. She said the women were all lying. They begged to see the doctor. Some slept on the doorstep of the clinic, hoping to convince him to fit them in. Others came clear across the state and handed over all of their money and bridal jewels. They knew what they were doing was illegal, and they didn't care. Everyone knew the police of the old country looked the other way. Even if they didn't, the women would have done it anyway. Anything to make sure their husbands got a son. That his family got an heir. The women said they were nothing if they couldn't produce—*reproduce*—on command. I guess that hasn't changed. The women of Koyanagar still want the same things. They've just made them harder to get.

I hang the dirty kurta on the hook and take out the fresh one. When I pull it over my head, the seams under the arms tear. I look over my shoulder. The guard says, "We ran out of large ones. Most of the boys are skinnier than you."

Skinny means starved. Appa says that when he was young, being skinny meant you were beautiful and glamorous and there were people who actually died because they got too good at being thin. Now skinny means poor and hungry, and no one wants to look like they're either. Some of the families starve themselves so they can fatten up their sons before their tests. This is like the market vendors who display their fruit shiny side up. They're hoping people will buy the fruit without turning it over, exactly like those parents are hoping the girls will pick their sons and marry them before they figure out that they don't know how to eat with three forks and drink tea from china cups. I don't understand the point of this deception. The girl will figure it out eventually. Why set the boys up to become even bigger disappointments than they already will be?

Appa didn't do anything to make me look different. We're lucky that we can grow our own food. Enough to feed ourselves and trade for other things at the market. Plus, we work eighteen hours a day. I can't help it if that has made me as strong and brown as an ox. A good thing for these physical tests, I suppose, but not a good one overall. That girl probably spends a fortune on powders so she can lighten her skin. Dark skin is equated with sunshine, and sunshine means outdoor work. She wouldn't want to appear like she isn't rich enough to avoid both.

I lean forward to retie my shoes and hear the fabric tear

clear across the back. The guard snickers. "Better put the old one back on, farm boy."

The boy in blue snorts from across the room. I shoot him a glare. His kurta fits as if it has been tailored for him. I bet we're supposed to believe that's a coincidence, just like we're supposed to believe it's a coincidence that he showed up for a secret football game with cleats and shin pads. The shin pads shouldn't surprise me, I guess. Appa says *the warrior who wears the armor is the one who's out for blood,* and there's no question that boy wants blood. Also no question he got it. From me, literally. From the young boy as well and his blood won't stop seeping here today. Unless he found a miracle cure for his broken leg, he'll be off to the assignment center with the crippled boy. By sundown, they'll both be at the wall and then . . .

No. I must not think of that. I cannot help them. They are beyond my control now.

I put the old kurta back on. It's cooler now and feels strangely refreshing, even though I know it's stained with grass, blood, and sweat. Whatever. I have no one to impress. This might even be better. The best thing for me would be if the girl believes I'm a useless market boy who doesn't care about the appearance of himself or his wife. A boy who would be an embarrassment to her and her family and who would sire more embarrassing boys. Then she definitely won't risk her future by giving me more rocks. She'll pick the boy most suited to be the father of her beautiful daughters, and that won't be a dirty savage like me.

Yes, the best thing for everyone is if I stick to the plan. I will forget about the boys who are gone. I will forget about the boys who are still here.

But most of all, I will forget about the girl.

SUDASA

20

The third Test's a race.
One
        mile to the finish.
One
        chance to show
        the stamina
        that's thought to produce
~~heirs~~ girls.

Thirty-two boys stand.
Solid glaciers in a line. The sun
        burning
their resolve. Daring them to stay
        afloat.

We girls watch from our boxes
like orchids in a greenhouse.
Sheltered
        from the past.
Blinded
        to the future.

Our focus is on the present—
a wood that's
        solid.

strong.
We don't see the veneer
that will soon
p
  e
   e
    l.
to Reveal
a truth rotted to the core.

The boys, equally as blind,
take their positions
on the track.
        Knees bent.
        Chins up.
        Fingers pressed into hot gravel.

When the gun lets out a
CRACK,
they burst from their line.
Whips of pressure
        sear
into hordes of desperate flesh.

Five doesn't burst.
He meanders instead.
He's slow enough
        to stay behind.
Fast enough
        to play the game.

Halfway around,
my third boy finds a
ho le.
He sprints ahead.
> Takes a lead.
> Takes a risk;
>> a risk too big.

My cousin leaves the pack,
a pretty boy by his side. They
> push hard.
> push ahead.
> push my third boy off the track.

He's on the ground.
A little bit hurt?
Maybe.
A lot more stunned.

To the others, he's a pylon
flattened
by a wheel.
Something to
> ignore.
> avoid.
> leave lying in its rightful place.

When Five reaches my third boy,
he stops on the track.
He extends
> a hand.

Gets nothing but warm
                    a i r
in return.

My third boy struggles to his feet
as if to say, *I'm all right,*
but when he tries to take a step,
his face contorts with pain.

Five takes his arm and
wraps it around his own shoulders.
                    He bears his weight.
                    Drags him forward.
                    Helps him do
what can't be done.

They're limp turtles as they continue,
far behind the pack of hares.
Pack of wolves is more like it.
                    And the rabbit?
That's me.

One lap in, they stop
within earshot of my box.
The third boy motions to the pack,
then says to Five,
"I don't stand a chance,
but you—you must not lose
because of me. These Tests
are important."

Five kind of shrugs
as if to say he
        doesn't agree.
        doesn't care.
        doesn't want me?

My third boy shakes his head,
his cheeks turning pink.
"If you won't do it for yourself,
do it for me or for that kid.
We'd both be running our hearts out
if that first boy hadn't stopped us."

That's all it takes.
The match is lit.
Five's fumes ignited.
His goal reset.

Although half a lap behind,
he takes off in a blaze,
his speed like the sun
in the cloudless sky.

Dropping her fan to her lap,
Nani lets out a gasp.
"That boy will never make it.
He shouldn't bother.
The Tests are done.
The winner clear."

I say, "Never say never,"
then I'm on my feet.

Matching her strength.
But my focus?
An unmatching boy.

The end of the second lap,
my cousin's way out front. He's
       drenched in sweat.
       drenched in confidence.
       drenched in the belief he's running alone.

He
       can't see behind him.
       can't see what we can.
       can't see Five pushing past
the front of the pack.

Nani jumps up,
her knuckles white
on the box's edge.
And while she manages to maintain a smile,
her *"Never"*
starts to m
      e
        l
          t.

Half a lap to go,
Five catches up.
He turns his head to my cousin.
Leaves him to answer
to his dust.

He races to the finish.
Arrives with the win sealed in his hand.
But before he steps over the line,
he sets it free,
        like a dove.

He gives a grand flourish
        as he steps to the side.
        as he motions *After you.*
Gives my cousin his victory.

He even
        waits for others.
        waits till they all cross the line. Even
        waits for my third boy
to find
not a disqualification
but still an end.

Nani starts to clap.
She believes my cousin has won.
Five more rocks gives him fifteen.
No other stands a chance.

Burning her seal on my shoulder,
she says, *"You may not like it,*
but you will learn.
He's a good boy."
And in a whisper she adds,
"His blood has girls."

I break the seal as I pull away.
Say, "The Tests aren't done."
And with a stare that matches her marble,
I make sure she knows:
Neither am I.

She grabs Mummy by the arm.
Says, *"You must talk to her, Nalini.*
Tell her it's better
to marry a rich boy.
Tell her why you chose
to do the same."

Mummy mouths, *"Chose?"*
as Papa turns away.
He drops his gaze to the ground,
his shame
        exposed—
                a crown of thorns.

She reaches for him
        as if she'll say,
It's all wrong.
        as if she'll say
she accepted his emerald ring because
        she loved him.
        loves him still.

But her hand goes limp
when she turns back to me,

cementing Nani's claim
that I was born from
           Coercion
and
           Obligation.

As the first girl gives her rocks,
Mummy pulls me into a hug.
She runs her hand
down my braid.
Finally offers some quiet advice.

"I know you think I don't understand,
but like you, I
had a choice at your age.

"Your mota masi presented me with two suitors:
           One a bit older and one near death.
           Both weighted with cash.
The older one said all the right things.
Showed your nani-ji the respect
she thought she deserved.

"As for the other one,"
Mummy adds with a grin,
"he was flashy and independent,
and he had more opinions
than she would have liked.

"Although I liked him better,
and knew he would make

a better husband for me,
truth be told,
I picked him to spite her.
For that, she has
never
forgiven me.

"You are not like me or your didi.
You never choose the best for yourself.
Never expect anyone to give it.

"And so I don't need to remind you
to play fair,
but today, with these Tests,
I do need to remind you
there's no point in being fair
to others
if you've forgotten to be fair
to yourself."

She lets go
as the director calls me forward
for my turn.

I take a step
but Nani stops me,
digging her nails into the sun
painted on my wrist.

"Your cousin won this Test.
That much is clear.

If you give your rocks to another,
you destroy what we've built
in Koyanagar."

I pull away with a vision
of my sister's baby—
the one who will never see life
if he's a boy.
The one who may join those baby girls
in the graves of History.

I say, "I'm sorry, Nani-ji,
but you've done that
on your own."

21

I move on to my three boys,
organized in a line.
Rules be damned,
I start
with second place first.

Handing two rocks to my third boy,
I say, "You knew you'd lost,
but still, you persevered.
That takes courage,
and in this life,
courage is gold."

I expect him to look distraught—
to realize his three rocks
leave him no chance—
and yet his outlook remains solid
even as its foundation
crumbles to dust.

I go to Five next,
five rocks in my hand.
When I put them in his,
I use my fingers
to close his fist.

He takes his other hand,
shrouding mine
like a kantha quilt.

"No," he whispers with a squeeze.
"Please don't."

I part my lips, the word "Why?"
dripping from my tongue.
I swallow it hard.
Feel an answer
thud
in my gut.

He's like me.
Forced to be here.
Forced to pay for mistakes not his.

But losing—
dying?—
that would be his.
Something
          he'd choose.
Something
          he'd own.

I want to show him
another choice.
That he can be proud
without death.

That he can be proud
<u>with me.</u>

Removing my hand, I say,
"Trust me.
I will help you.
I promise."

I move on to my cousin,
stopping a safe distance
from his tentacles.

He steps out of line.
Leans toward my cheek.
Says, *"I knew you'd be mine."*

His finger brushes my neck.
I pull back with
      a flinch.
      a tightened jaw.
      a clenched fist.

Test or no Tests,
I am not his.
I do
NOT
belong to anyone.
Only belong
to me.

When he holds out his palm,
I let drop a single rock. He
         waits for the others.
         waits for the victory
not his.

When I step away, he snaps,
"Sudasa, hold on.
I won that race fair and square.
You saw me cross that line."

I want to explain the meaning of "fair."
Want to scold him for saying my name.
For implying we're more than
         contestant
and
         prize.

With a flash of my palms,
I let Papa's Blake speak instead.
"Don't you remember,
Contestant One?
'The eye altering, alters all.'"

His love for poetry
becomes a sham
with sharp words and a frown.
"Which means what?"

I am without a plan,
but flash a grin nevertheless.

"Which means you see what you want,
and you want what you see,
and if I have anything
to say about it,
that will
never
be
me."

22

In the carriage, Nani is silent,
and yet her anger is
loud.
It yells in her frown.
SCREAMS!
when she exhales too hard.

Surina gives me the kind of look
only an older sister can give.
The one that's part
I know better
and all
I told you so.

When we pull up to our building,
Nani scurries past
Surina's husband.
I half expect her to tip him
for holding the door.
Wouldn't be his first bribe,
that's for sure.

Papa remains in his seat,
even after Surina and Mummy
are gone.

His fingers are twisted on his lap,
brown and gnarled
like an old banyan tree.

He looks like he wants to
speak,
but like the tree,
his tongue has grown
knots.

I move to the seat by his side.
"Papa," I say,
"do you think I should pick him?"

He continues to twist his fingers.
Raises his eyes.
Says, *"Your nani-ji—"*

I stomp the rules by yelling, "Nai!
I'm asking you.
Not her.
Tell me, do
you
think I should do
what Nani says?"

It takes him a moment
to free
      the chains from his tongue;
to remember the time,
      twelve years ago,
when he was allowed an opinion of his own.

When he speaks, he says,
"A man is measured
not by the answers he finds
but the questions he asks.
Find an answer
and you stand still.
Stop asking questions
and you die."

Although full of poetic words,
his answer contains none
that tell me what to do.
So I ask him once again,
"Papa, who should I choose?"

With a shake of his head,
he says, *"That's an answer*
I cannot bestow,
but if you look inside yourself,
I think you'll find
you already know."

      I already know?
            I already know?

I already
      know I won't marry my cousin.
      know I don't want to marry a stranger instead. I
      know there's a boy not so strange—
a boy named
Five?—

but he wants
freedom,
not the tether of a wedding ring.

I know I have no options.
At least none
my heart tells me to pick.

I need a different heart
to become my voice.
One that knows how to choose
between a rock
and a stone.
One like—
Asha.
Yes!
Asha.

She was in my place
two weeks ago. She was
forced to choose among five mangoes
when all she wanted was an orange.

She'll tell me what to do.
Asha *always* knows
what to do.

Papa and I go inside.
I squirm in silence
as we wait for the lift
to return to the ground.

"Papa," I say
with an apology in my voice,
"I need to see Asha.
It's not—
What you said—
But I think—
She has been through this and—"

Papa shushes me
with a finger in front of his lips.

When the lift arrives,
he answers my request
by pressing
the button for her floor.

I thank him with a hug.
Wish custom hadn't taught me knots.
Wish it had taught me
how
to say *I love you.*
Wish it had taught me
how
to say even more.

23

I get out on Asha's floor.
Kick off my shoes.
I head
        straight for her flat.
        straight for her room.
        straight for her arms.

My eyes well up like clouds
on the precipice of a monsoon.
Asha remains the stoic mountain.
        Unmoving.
        Unchanging.

"How did you do it?" I ask her
when I find my voice.
"How did you choose a stranger
when the boy you love
must compete for someone else?"

She sits on her bed.
Pats the silk cover.
I sit, too.

"My choice was easy," she says.
"The boys in my Tests were all strangers.

I concentrated on the game and
awarded the winner."

"But this is not like when we used
to play Tests with our dolls," I say.
"You must marry this winner
in ten days.
Does it not break your heart
to walk away
from what might have been?"

She twirls the end of her braid
around her fingers,
the way she used to twirl the boy she loves
around her life.

"I always knew he wouldn't be on my stage.
Maybe that made it easier?
He had my heart,
and you can't break
what you don't have."

"But my heart's still mine,"
I say, shaking my head.
Wondering if it's true.
If, like the other women in my family,
I don't even have one.
"And if my Nani makes me
marry my cousin—"

Asha's mouth opens
before her words

have the chance to fill it.
"Your cousin's in your Tests?
But that's statistically—"

"Impossible?"
I say with a head tilt.
"Apparently, anything's possible
if you're my nani."

She pauses to do the math—
something she's better at than me.

Her eyes get clear
when she sums up the reality:
   statistics don't matter
   to people who cheat.

With her chin held high,
Asha gives her decree.
"You'll pick someone else.
Your nani may be
the Puppet Master of State,
but she's not yours and
she can't make you
marry that louse."

I drop my gaze.
Say, "Nai. She can't,
and I would defy her if . . ."

When I don't finish,
Asha leans in

as if she can smell the
rest of my words
on my breath.
"If what?" she says.

I exhale like a punctured balloon.
"Two of my boys were disqualified,
which leaves my cousin
and two others:
one who's desperate to be chosen
but doesn't stand a chance,
and another who could win
but is desperate to lose."

I pause.
Consider my options.
Provide my own response.

"I know what you're thinking.
I must pick him anyway.
Must show him how good his life will be
with me.
Then he'll be happy.
Right?"

Asha frowns.
"You sound like your nani
at the dinner table.
Always telling people
they need more food
even if their stomachs are full."

I shake my head.
"Nai.
It's not like that."
I'm not like that.
Am I?
No.
Five's life would be better with me.
I'm sure of it.

Asha goes to the window,
staring through the bars
at the brick building
a few feet away.

"You have another choice, Susa,"
she says so low I wonder
if she's talking to the windowpane.
"You can choose not to marry.
Choose to leave Koyanagar
for good."

Her suggestion is a rabbit
magically pulled from a hat.
I want to believe it's possible,
but reason tells me
it's not.

I tell her, "There's no way.
Even if I could escape,
I can't leap across the sea.
And the wall—

even if I could leap over that,
it's a jungle on the other side.
I'd be food for sharks
of one kind
or another."

She turns back to me with a torque
so powerful
it whips her braid off her shoulder.

For the first time in our lives,
I see Asha
            clench her teeth.
            narrow her eyes.
            spit her words.

"That's a lie
your nani puts on your spoon
so you'll think you stay here
by choice.

"The wall's a bunch of rocks,
and the people on the other side are
neither
sharks nor fools
like us.

"Traffic goes one way,
and it's out.
That's why they keep sending

more boys to the wall.
They're escaping,
and no one cares."

"But I'm not a boy,"
I say, pulling at my sheer dupatta
as if she'll be surprised to see it.
"They'll care if I leave.
And when my nani finds out—"

Asha glances at an old canvas bag tucked
between
her bed
and side table.
"What if you weren't
a girl when you crossed?" she says,
returning her braid to her fingers.
"What if you had scissors? Clothes?
Papers that said you were a boy
and had permission to leave?"

When she looks at the bag again,
I realize we're not
talking about me
anymore.

I glance toward the hall,
lowering my voice.
"Have you forgotten what happened
to that girl
who ran away four years ago?

The one whose boyfriend
refused to participate in the Tests?
Who refused to tell where
she was hiding unless State
promised they could marry?

"They didn't punish only him.
They punished his parents
and hers.
They took away their endowment.
Threw them out on the street."

Asha shakes her head.
Says, *"My parents don't care.*
They didn't have
an arranged marriage like yours.
They married for love.
Don't believe there's any other way.

"They gave me hope in my name.
They took the yira for my wedding
and told me to use it
to buy my own happiness."

I want to believe
in her magic,
and yet something about it
still smells like an empty hat.

"But what if you're wrong?"
I say cautiously,

because Asha's
not the kind of girl
who gets things wrong.
And yet, she's also
not the kind of girl
who takes risks—
is she?

"What if life on the outside
is worse than it is here?"
I ask her.

She returns to her place next to me.
"Then I'll still be unhappy,
but I'll have chosen that misery,
and that's the only way
I can win."

I want to tell her not to go.
Not to take the risk.
Not to leave me the lone bird
in a field of cats.

But I can't.
She has love
and she has hope and
I can't take that away.
Can't ask her to abandon it
so she can stay in a nation
that breaks its own laws.
Its own people.

She takes my hand.
"You could come with me," she says.
"We'll ask my baaba to buy more papers.
Cut your hair like mine.
We'll share my money until we're settled.
Then we'll find jobs.
Maybe even a boy for you, too?"

I give her a hug,
but I say, "Nai.
I will miss you"—
            so, so much—
"but this is
            your plan,
            your money,
            your future"—
            your choice—
"and it's about time
I find one of my own."

CONTESTANT FIVE

24

I'm back in my cement cell. Alone again. Probably a good thing. I have always had Appa around. At home. In the fields. At the market. But after tomorrow, I'm on my own. No one to work with or eat with or laugh with or be silent with. Not until I find Amma. *If* I find Amma. Appa drew me a map of the old country. Who knows if it's still the same. The only things we hear about it are what we're told in the Koyanagar newspaper, and it portrays everyone there as miserable. It says they're starving to death on the street, killing each other so they can stay alive. It says they would do anything—risk anything—to find a better place to call home. As far as I can tell, the only difference between them and us is they admit their country is falling apart, while our leaders honestly believe they've created some kind of utopia. It's like Appa says, *the people at the top of the pyramid always think the sun shines the brightest.*

I take the rocks out of my pocket and toss them on the young boy's cot. *Former* cot. Five more rocks. How can I have five more rocks? This was not part of the plan. I pace back and forth from the door to the wall. Door to the wall. Door to the— No, no, no, no, no. I can't have these rocks. I can't be in second place, two days in and with only two other boys left, one of whom has zero chance of beating the boy in blue. Worse, I can't let this girl believe that giving me these rocks is somehow helping me. She probably believes she can solve all my problems by giving me a luxurious life, but it's *her* life and I want my own. How can I tell her that? How can I make her see that she needs to be with that disgusting boy who touched her neck like he'd already won and then said her name as if it was forty years ago and he was the one with the money and the power and the influence?

Sudasa. It means obedience. Being obedient would mean picking the boy in blue—the one her family clearly wants. I saw the way her grandmother shot ocular daggers at her when she awarded me the five rocks. She doesn't want someone like me in her home, looking at her expensive art and touching her silk cushions. Not to mention living with the poster girl for Koyanagar. How would that look? The girl everyone idolizes with a brother-in-law whose own mother didn't love him enough to stay.

Surely, they will make Sudasa see this tonight. They will tell her I won't fit in. Then they will remind her of her duty as a girl. They will think for her, as they always do, because that's the point of these tests. If they could trust the girls to choose wisely on their own, we wouldn't have to be here. Would we? Or is it the opposite? Perhaps the families have always chosen for them and the key is to let the girls decide for themselves?

No. No. No. That's exactly what she did when she gave *me* the five rocks.

I sit on my cot, placing my head in my hands. If only I could talk to Appa. He'd know what to do. He'd remind me why his plan is the only option. Why becoming the husband of a rich girl is a bad thing, even if it would guarantee that he would always have food and water and the kind of medicine that might finally make his stomach better. Not that he wants these things. We talked about this before—when I asked him if he would prefer it if I married—and he said it was my turn to be happy. If he can deplete his savings and break the law for me, the least I can do is trust that he knows best.

No, I cannot let him down. Not for a pretty girl whose gaze is like Tagore's sad depth of the sky. It's not even like she has lost hope. I see that in the market all the time, mostly with the older men who come to talk to Appa about what life was like before everything changed. For her, it's almost like she doesn't know what hope is. Like she has accepted that this life in Koyanagar is the only option.

I jump to my feet and pace again. Door, cot, wall, cot, door. Why can't she see that accepting this way of life is not the only option? Why can't she think for herself for once? Wait. No, we're back at the same problem. She can't do that. Thinking for herself is what made her pick me, and she can't pick me.

I sit back down. I must stop thinking about her and her eyes and her delicate painted wrists. I must stick to the plan. Amma is out there somewhere. Could I live with myself if I never tried to find her. If I never got the chance to ask her why she left? Could I drink from crystal goblets knowing that Appa gave up everything in order to give me the chance for a better life? And could I ever look him in the eyes again if I did?

I tear off my dirty red kurta, replacing it with the T-shirt I was wearing when the guards took me from my home. I inhale as it brushes over my cheeks. Salt. It smells of sea salt, and the sea means freedom for me. But it also means home and comfort and a life of not being alone. No. I must forget about that. I must focus on <u>the plan.</u>

I lie down and close my eyes. The lightbulb buzzes, although not nearly as loud as my head. Pictures whir around my skull like a nest of angry bees. The farm. Her eyes. The wall. The sea. Appa. Amma. Me. The girl.

I take a long, deep breath. Tomorrow. I will find a way to stop her from choosing me. I will fail every test. I won't give her a choice. She may not like it, but she will learn to. And perhaps the boy in blue won't be so bad once he has won. Perhaps her family will keep him in his place. Yes, it will work. She will pick him, and I will lose in the final test, exactly like Appa planned.

But if it doesn't work—if she still tries to pick me—I'll beg her not to. I'll find a way to bribe her, to persuade her.

And if that doesn't work, I'll forget what Appa said about the dangers of trying to get away while the tests are still going and everyone is looking at me. I'll start the plan early.

I'll run.

DAY THREE

SUDASA

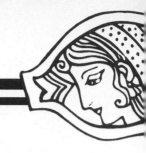

25

The final day.
Two Tests left.
Next up:
practical skills.

Skills like Papa has needed
since he was deemed
not good enough—
        not female enough—
to teach literature.

They'd rather give the job
        to a middle-aged woman—
        one who has barely skimmed Tagore—
than let a man mold our minds.

When we arrive at the venue,
we're ushered down the stone path.
Told to step around
the hundreds of bikes
        bleeding from rust.
        piled like bones in a mass grave.

We're told to plug our noses
to escape the smells.

Manure.
Rot.
Poverty?
Reality.

We enter an old building
crammed
between two modern towers.

Nani says it used to be a
men's club.
A place her husband
came home from smelling of
Scotch.
paan.
lavender perfume.

Now they use it for the final Tests.
Give the ties that bind
in the place that used to
set them free.

My family sits at a round table
declared to be mine
by the embossed center card:
Miss Sudasa Bala
Keeper of the Rocks?
More like
Ambassador of the Deaths.

Sitting straight in her seat,

Nani keeps her neck taut
like a rooster on its perch.

I let my neck recoil
into my feathers
as eyes
drip down its side.

The eyes are from the boys' families.
Their fingertips are
            pressed against the windows.
Their hope
            diminishing as the clock ticks by.

There's silence when the director enters.
A different woman, yet
            still old.
            still unadorned in white.
            still sporting a smile for Nani.

The boys—
what's left of the boys . . .
twenty, maybe twenty-five in total?—
huddle in eight small groups
at the front of the room.

They keep their chins at attention as
the director reads off the assignments.
The lucky ones, like group #2,
are sent down the hall
to clean.

The less fortunate, like group #5,
are sent out back
to do repairs.

My boys are assigned cooking,
so my choice is not
transparent glass
like it is for the other girls.

I must decide.
Must pretend I didn't spend the
W H O L E N I G H T
tossing.
            turning.
                        waking to smudge and *smear*.

When my boys are sent to the kitchen
to prepare their offering,
I'm left to
w
a
i
t.

w
o
n
d
e
r.

t
h
i
n
k.

Nani drums her fingers
on the yellow tablecloth,
her foot tapping her chair's leg
with every fourth beat.

Mummy keeps refilling
her full water glass,
taking small sips in between,
like it's chai, steaming hot.

Papa has his book satchel on his lap.
He stares at the same page of a cookbook,
his eyes a glossy costume
meant to show
he's here
while his mind drifts away.
          Away to somewhere better.
          Somewhere he'd rather be?

After an hour,
I'm sent to the kitchen
          to taste.
          to judge.
          to decide.

Nani tells Surina
to go along as my chaperone.
She grudgingly follows behind
me like a shadow.
(Not a silent one.)

The moment we open the kitchen door
and swallow the scent of fish,
Surina smothers her complaints
with her palm,
taking off for the bathroom.

In the kitchen,
I find several cooking areas,
my third boy in the first.
His meal—
          his future?—
a pile of charcoal
smoking in his hands.

"*It used to be mackerel,*" he says,
placing the plate on the counter.
"*I suppose I'm done.
That first boy has eleven rocks
to my three.*"

I expect him to finally show
his defeat, but
he smiles at the blackened lump
and says, "*It's all right.
My sister will buy me a future—*

though perhaps as a coachman,
not a cook."

I feel a weight in my heart
for this sweet, gentle boy,
but I'd like to set him free,
not call him my husband.

I add one rock to his collection.
As I step away, I tell him,
"You'll be a great addition
to some girl's home."
And I hope, for his sake,
that *some girl* thinks so, too.

I continue to the second part of the kitchen—
the one with familiar smells
floating in the air.

My cousin stands at the counter,
a knife and fork in one hand,
a plate of oysters in coconut cream
in the other.

He chose this dish because it creates acid,
and acid creates girls,
and he wants me to know
he will also do this.

He pierces the rubbery flesh.
Holds it out on the fork.

Waits for me to let him
shove his proof
down my throat.

I snatch the fork from his hand.
Take a small bite
on my own.

There's no question it's good.
It should be.
I bet it's the same recipe
Nani tells Surina's husband
to make every week.

When my cousin opens his hand,
I place two rocks on the counter.
I say: "I'll be back if you deserve the other three."
I know: he doesn't deserve even one.

He grabs my elbow,
hissing, *"Sudasa,"*
like my name's a swear.

I scowl at his hand.
Say, "I could leave you
with one instead."

He pulls me close against his chest.
His breath—a dragon's.
His eyes—a snake's.
"You're just trying to make me sweat," he says.

"Trying to show me who's boss.
Don't you worry.
You'll be the one sweating
in our marriage bed."

I push him away,
and without even thinking,
I slap him
across the face.

He laughs,
          as if this is all a game.
          as if my hating him
sprinkles sugar
on his victory.

Maybe it does.
I would not be his prey
if I didn't want
to run
away.

26

I rush around the corner,
past the exit door.
I duck into the bathroom.
Grab the sides of the washbasin to
            steady my heart.
            steady my nerves.
            steady my thoughts.

My stomach churns at the thought
of calling my cousin
            Husband.
But it churns more at the thought
of forcing Five to take his place
instead.

Could I really be happy
living like a horse whisperer?
Using a palm full of oats
to entice my hostage
from the corner of his corral,
my fingers curled by the fear
of being bitten?

No.
I am <u>not</u> Nani.

I will **not** take prisoners
in my own home.

Staring into the mirror,
I
tell my tears to stop.
tell myself to stay
STRONG.
And I do until
I find Five in the kitchen—
a pillar
to my puddle.

He leans against a gleaming counter.
No smells.
No dishes.
No evidence he has touched a thing.

No.
How can he do this to me?
How can he leave me with only one choice?
One I don't want.

My eyes become pools,
and before I can ask him
why he hasn't started,
in his low voice
he says,
*"You need not worry.
I finished long ago."*

I look around.

"Do you have an offering?" I ask,
my voice cracking.

With a nod, he replies,
"Like the darkness,
it will appear when you close your eyes."

I bite through a smile.
Shut my eyes.
Wait for his magic.

He speaks again.
"You must open your mouth, too."

I open my mouth and
his fingers
brush my lips
like a ghost.

His offering sits
in the middle of my tongue.
Cold.
Tasteless.

I bite it.
Prepare to hate it.
Because that's what he wants.
        Right?

That will
        force me to give
        three more rocks to my cousin.

That will
        end these Tests.
        give him a one-way ticket out of here.

The moment my teeth pierce
the soft flesh of the sphere,
a sour juice
tickles
my tongue.

It's the taste of the forbidden;
                forbidden
from my home
because it will neutralize
the same kind of acid
my cousin tried to create.

I had one once. Years ago.
Papa said he got it from Hun Market.
At the time, I thought he meant
the illegal part. The part
everyone knows about
but no one ever discusses.

Later, I learned that girls
ate them all the time.
Other girls. Girls
whose grandmothers
weren't obsessed with
filling their homes
with more girls.

I open my eyes.
Say, "They're my favorite.
But you didn't cook it.
That was the Test."

Five grins.
"The rules say we must make you
something to eat.
I dug a hole in my land
and grew that myself."

With a smile bursting from my lips,
I reach into my pocket.
I want to give him all five rocks.
Want to tell him he
        won.
        won my favor.
        won me?

He shakes his head,
reminding me
I am not the prize he seeks.
"That cherry was payment," he says,
"for my freedom."

The churn in my stomach swells
to a tidal wave.
"But I can't marry my cousin.
I'd rather die than—
Please, let me pick you.
Then you can go live your life.

I'll make excuses.
Pretend we're together.
It'll work."
         It has to.

He steps back to his corner,
shaking his head.
"I won't be forced to be a husband,
just as you don't want to be forced to be a wife."

I pause to find another option.
"What if I pick you
but you leave before the wedding?"

Another step.
"Then the people of Koyanagar will think
you weren't good enough for a farm boy."

I keep my eyes lowered as I reply.
"But that is true. I am not good enough
to make you stay."

His eyes grow wide and yet
no words
fill his open mouth.

"It's true," I say again.
"You'd rather die than be married to me.
And you will die if you lose.
You'll be sent to the wall
and I'll be forced to live

with the burns from your noose
on my palms."

Five rips the mask
off his face,
flinging it
on the stainless counter.

"Do you call this living—
competing for life in a cage?
I don't.
It's death in slow motion.
It's the same at the wall,
although death, for some, comes quicker.

"Well, I don't want death.
I want life.
I want a job
          I choose.
A home
          I choose.
A wife
          I choose.
And not in Koyanagar."

His eyes are soft
under thick eyebrows,
but there's no question
his words are steel.

He wants to leave
and nothing I say—
or do—
will stop him.

When I see the gleam
of hope in his eyes,
I realize—
        honestly?—
I don't want to.

I want to
        cut off the lock.
        open the gate.
        remove his bridle.
        set him free.

Like Asha, he knows what he wants,
and he has a chance
to grasp it.
I won't take that away,
even if it means
I have no chance
for myself.

"I can help you," I say.
"You'll need money to cross the wall and—"

He holds up his hand.
"No.

The wall is lined
by a moat of piranhas.
I don't want to be
their dinner."

"But I know someone," I say,
swallowing Asha's name
and gender.
"Someone who said you can get through
with yira and—"

"A disguise?" he says,
pointing at his mask.
"That rumor is cheese used to catch the sneaky mouse.
It's a lie.
No one gets through.
The men at the wall have no use for money.
They want revenge.
Blood. Anyone's blood.
Boys.
Girls?
Even better."

I step back,
my hands—my voice—shaking.
"Nai, it can't be.
My friend was sure there's a way out."

His voice is calm when he says,
"There is, but not by land."

"You mean by boat?"

He grins. *"'You can't cross the sea*
merely by standing and staring at the water.'
Tell your friend if she wants
to find the land of the free,
she'd better grow some fins."

"But—"

"Trust me," he says,
hovering his warm fingers
in front of my lips.
Piercing my eyes with a look
so convincing
he could tell me to jump
off Agnimar Cliff
and my only question would be
Should I go head- or feetfirst?

He drops his hand as he continues.
"Like yours, my future was decided
twelve years ago
and that's a lot of time for research.

"The people who lose their sons
in these Tests—
many have tried to follow them:
            to make sure they're alive.
            to try to steal them back.
But there are only two

kinds of boys at the wall:
        those who kill and
        those who are killed.
And neither returns home."

I drop five rocks on the counter.
My hand
        shaking.
My mind
        sinking
in a quicksand made of a
million
tiny
particles,
each one an image of Asha
at the wall.

No.
She was supposed to be here.
Before I left her flat last night,
I made her promise that wasn't
our goodbye.
Made her promise she'd come
to my Choosing Ceremony.

Five pushes the rocks toward me.
His eyes are desperate when he says,
"No. Please, please don't.
I must leave before the Choosing Ceremony is done.
My amma—I need to find my amma.

"Her name was Veera Pillai,"
he adds as if he needs
to offer proof.
*"She left the night they closed
the gates.
This is my last chance
to see her again."*

That's when I see the longing
in his eyes.
He isn't running from someone—
someone like me.
He's running to someone.
To his mother.

I say, "I promise I will help you.
But if I don't give those to you now,
these Tests are done
and I'm not ready for that.
I need some more time
to fulfill your request.
Some more time to find
some other . . .
options."

But what I need first
is to find Asha
fast,
or I won't be
the only one
with a sealed fate.

27

On my way out of the kitchen,
I dip my fingers in some ginger chutney.
I smear it across my right sleeve.
Prepare a wound
        for my battle.

When I return to the table,
Nani puts down her spoon,
letting it ping against the china
like a timer at its finish.

"You're done?" she says,
and she doesn't mean
with the fourth Test.

Pointing at my stained choli, I say,
"I need to go home to change."

She glares at my dupatta
as if she can will it to move
from my left shoulder
to my right.

Even if she could,
the stain would still show.

The chiffon is as sheer
as her smiles.

I don't have time to argue,
so I distract her
with a juicy bone.

"Do you want me to choose my husband
looking like this?
Mota Masi will think we're
too poor
for clean clothes."

My bone turns Nani
into a grinning hound.
"Go," she says,
waving me away,
drips of victory glistening
on her jowls.
"Come back in something nice."

Then, removing the key
from around her neck,
she adds, *"You can wear
my ruby drops, since it's a
special occasion."*

I snatch the key from her hand,
rushing to the exit
before she figures out
what I've done.

When I get into the carriage,
I instruct the coachman
to drive as if
his life depends on it.
Because someone's does.

I become an athlete
when we arrive at the building.
      Sprinting
across the sidewalk
in my stiff beaded shoes.
      Racing
to the lift, heart
beat
beat
beating
as I wait for the next race.

A minute later,
I'm at Asha's flat.
Don't need to knock.
Her baaba's standing in the open door.

"I'm looking for Asha," I say,
glancing around.
Trying not to panic
at the boxes rising from every corner
like blocks ready to topple.

My head tells me

this is only for show.
Act I: Make room for Asha's husband.

But my heart knows
this is all too real.
There are too many boxes.
Not enough life.

"She's not here," her baaba says.
His face droops like a wrinkled apple
and I can tell by the red in his eyes
that he doesn't mean
for now.
"Shouldn't you be at the club?" he asks.

I point to my shoulder,
too dazed to be sure
I've picked the one with the stain.
"I had to change," I say.
"I guess I'll see her at my ceremony."

I turn back toward the lift,
not waiting to see if he'll
confirm.
Knowing it might be a lie
even if he did.

In my room, I pull out the sari
I wore to Surina's wedding.
I run my fingers over one of the

embroidered suns
that were added for good luck.

They were a little too late
for Surina.
Hopefully, not
too late
for me.

I lay the sari on my bed.
See an envelope
poking out from under my bear
like a child up past bedtime.

I pull it out and my heart
               STOPS
when I see Susa
in Asha's *loopy* handwriting.

She has no reason to
write me a letter.
Not if she's coming to my ceremony.
And she must come
to my ceremony.

She.
Must.

I unfold the page,
and my eyes race to the end

as if their speed
can catch her words
before they come true.

Susa,
I hope you understand
why I couldn't stay.
The place where I'm going
will always have a hole
up high where you should be.
I hope you find
what you're looking for.
Love, A.

I read it two more times.
Don't want to accept
that she's gone.
She can't be.

Not before I tell her what Five said
       about the sea.
       about the wall.
       about the revenge.

I fold my sari around my waist.
Continue as planned. Ignore
the
       fist in my stomach.
the
       tempest in my head.

This is it.
Act II: Pretend everything's fine.

I go to Nani's room.
Take the key.
Open the safe.

The jewels' plush red box
is near the back—
its companions,
rolls of the
old country's money.

I figure these are keepsakes,
like the antique mobile phone
that's tucked in there also.
But when I pull out a roll,
I see
           the old wrinkled face
           of the great Gandhi-ji
           and
           a date, not old at all.

No.
It can't be.
Koyanagar created the yira
when it formed.

How would Nani get
banknotes from last year?
Why

would Nani get
banknotes from last year?

Unless—

Could this be how she buys her way
around the system?
Could this mean
          that Five got it wrong?
          that it *is* possible to cross the wall
if you have the
right
kind of money?

That maybe,
if I had that kind of money,
I could find Asha?
Help her get across?
Go with her?

That maybe
I could help Five, too.
Help him find ~~what~~ who he lost.
Help him win something from this game.

I take the roll and box.
Search for the Koyanagar Registry—
the hard black book
that should be tucked behind it all.

I've seen Nani take it from here.
Often moments after a courier arrives

with news:
        Sometimes happy.
        Oftentimes not.

I rummage around,
but the book is gone
and so is the sand
in my hourglass.

I rush to the kitchen
for a knife.
I stuff it in my bag
with Papa's old clothes.
Wish I had some courage
to pack instead.

Could this be it?
Act III: Trudge ahead?
Without
        sight?
Without
        plans?
Without
        a hope in hell?

When the carriage returns me
to the stone building,
I find Nani pacing,
her face ready to burst
like an overcooked tomato.

"You awarded that—
that oaf again. You said—"
She exhales hard,
glaring at the jewels
on my ears and neck.

"Those jewels are
mine.
They belong in
my
family. Maybe you need to remember
that you also
belong there."

"Don't worry," I tell her
with a confidence I don't feel.
"Everyone will end up
exactly where they belong
in the end."

That's Act IV:
Decide where that will be
for me.

28

I sit in the waiting room, my elbows resting on my knees. The boy in blue demanded that the guard take him to see the director of the test. He's probably trying to convince her I cheated somehow. I didn't, but I still shouldn't have given the girl a cherry from my bag. I should have stuck to the plan and told her I didn't know how to cook, even though Appa has taught me how to season lentils and chop ginger until it's as fine as dust.

But tears. Tears. I couldn't ignore her tears and the way she looked so desperate to get away from him. He must have done something awful. Something worse than when he touched her. Something that proves he will never change and doesn't deserve her or any girl. But now it's down to him and me and she has to choose one of us and if it's not me it's—

No. I can't let her do that. I wouldn't be able to live with myself knowing I forced her into his clutches. But what else can I do? I have to stick to the plan. Appa said the only way for me to escape unnoticed is if I do it while everyone is distracted during the Choosing Ceremony. There will be a few minutes between when I'm sent off the stage and when the guards have to collect all the other losers for transfer to the assignment center. If I don't get away then, I'll be sent to the wall and it will be almost impossible to escape. Yes, I must stick to the plan. Appa said the boat would be waiting in the barn and I need to be out to sea before there's enough light for the shoreline patrol guards to spot me. Then I will be gone from Koyanagar for good and I will never look back, just like I promised Appa. He will tell everyone I threatened to jump off Agnimar Cliff if I lost and they will all assume this is what happened. I will get work in the old country and then I will search for Amma. The girl—Sudasa—will marry the boy and she will be rich and comfortable like the rest of the girls in Koyanagar. But when I leave, I won't think about that. I will forget her and her sad eyes and her awful future.

Won't I?

But what if it is like with Amma? What if I spend my whole life wondering what happened to her? And what if she spends her whole life feeling like me? Feeling like the lone shoe left behind the cart? I have to tell her she is better than that.

I press my forehead into my hands.

No. She is not my responsibility. I must forget her. I must focus on my new life outside Koyanagar. My life that will start with Amma telling me it was all a misunderstanding. She didn't want to leave Koyanagar but she got caught up in the crowds that were pushing through the gate. Or she meant to leave but was planning to come back before the gates were closed but then there was a delay and she couldn't get back in. Or she thought Appa would change his mind and we'd come with her when the gates opened again. She didn't know they'd still be closed twelve years later. One of these must be true.

And as soon as I find out which one it is, I will have my wheel back and will be able to move my wheelbarrow forward into my future.

There's a light rap on the door. I look up as a man enters. It's not the guard. This man is wearing a long gray kurta with white chikan decorating the collar. The cotton is crisp and freshly pressed. A sign that his home has servants. Or that he's one of them? But why would he be here? And why does he seem so familiar?

He sits on the bench next to me, placing a black satchel on the floor next to his pointy jutis. "You are from Mannipudi," he tells me as if he knows this is a fact.

I nod anyway.

"I suppose they don't call it that now that it has been swallowed by Koyanagar. Is it still very different from the big city? Does it still have that man Anand? The old boat maker who sells his carved elephants at Hun Market?"

I nod again. Is that where I know him from? He's a buyer at the market? Should I be worried that he mentioned Anand? Appa refused to tell me who helped him with his plan, including who made the boat I'm using to escape. He said it was better if I knew only what I had to do. That way, if I was caught and questioned by the army, they couldn't beat me into betraying those people who had risked their necks to help Appa.

"You have your appa's eyes. I think, perhaps, his spirit, also." The man adds a grin and then motions to the bridge of my nose—the part that's still a bit red and swollen from yesterday. "The boy with the glass nose. I suppose your appa was right about that!"

I scrunch my forehead. "You know my appa from the market?"

The man stares ahead as if his mind has left for a journey yet his body has stayed behind. "Yes, yes," he says, returning his focus to me. "We have much in common these days. But I also knew your appa when I was younger. Or, at least, he knew me. He used to watch me play cricket. The people from Mannipudi—like that man Anand—they say he was my greatest fan. Some say I owe at least part of my fame and fortune to your appa."

My eyes become full moons. "You are *the Mighty Bala*? But why—" I clip the rest of my sentence. I want to ask him why Appa didn't point him out at the market and if he still plays cricket, but I have no right to question a man like him. And if he's here, I already know most of the answers. There is no cricket in Koyanagar. No more glory for sport—for men.

The Mighty Bala stands. "He's a wise man, your appa. He does not alter when alteration he finds, nor bend with the remover to remove. . . . Ah, there I go again. Letting my words carry me away." He shakes his head and adds, "Even at the darkest hour, your appa knows the right path to follow. You must trust this."

I say, "Yes, Uncle," as I kneel down to touch his feet, bowing my head and closing my eyes. It may no longer be custom in Koyanagar, but this man has Appa's deepest respect and he deserves mine, as well.

My eyes are still closed when I remember where I saw him before. He was seated at the yellow table when I received the instructions for my last test. The table with the ice water and the sad girl named Sudasa. Could he be her father? Could the man Appa can't forget have created the girl I must? But why would he come in here and tell me that I must follow Appa's plan no matter what? Could he actually want his daughter to marry a monster?

I'm about to stand so I can ask him this when I notice his satchel on the floor. I look up, my lips already parted to remind him not to forget it. But I don't get to speak before I realize he's gone.

I jump to my feet. I'm not supposed to leave the room, but I'm sure I can catch him in the hallway if I lean out the door. I grab the handle of the satchel, and a hard black book falls out, splaying on the floor like a dropped melon. I pick it up. It's a list of names arranged by year. A directory? Or . . . could this be it—the famous Koyanagar Registry? But why would *the Mighty Bala* have it? And why would he leave it here with me, the poor boy who is trying *not* to win his daughter's hand in marriage?

I flip through the yellowed pages until I find the section for 2036. I scan through the months of birth . . .

August . . .

September . . .

October . . . there it is!

I locate my name. Next to it, in the same black ink, is my citizenship number and date of birth—2 October. There's a blank space where my date of death will go one day, perhaps soon. Who knows what they will put when I disappear. Probably the date I supposedly jumped off the cliff (in red, of course). There's a circled blue *T* in the margin by my name. I scan the other pages in 2036 and see this same symbol next to many other boys' names. This must be how they know we've been selected for the tests.

I scan back a couple more years. The blue *T*'s are random and not nearly as common as the red dates of death. Could this be what *the Mighty Bala* wanted me to see? The reality of what will happen to me if I don't follow the plan?

The pounding of my heart grows to a dull thud and I'm washed with the feeling that *the Mighty Bala* might have wanted me to see something else. Something worse.

I continue to flip back until I get to 2004 and then I scan the months until I find Appa's name: *Pillai, R. Maani.* I let out a deep breath when I see that his date of death is still blank. I know I saw him only a few days ago. Still, I can't help but worry. He's not well and he will die one day. It may be when I'm working at my new job or when I'm eating or asleep. I won't know when it happens. I won't know if it's in a week or in a year or in ten years.

The pounding in my chest morphs into a sharp pain. There's another name I must see before I return the satchel to *the Mighty Bala.* I flip forward to 2013, locate April, and then scan down the days.

1 April.

3 April.

7 April.

The pain in my chest disappears. It's replaced with something hard and dry, like a lump of clay that has been left out in the air. There's a Veera Pillai with Amma's birth date, 11 April. But in the column next to it, there's no blank. There's a second date: 31 December 2041. It's the day before they closed the Koyanagar gates. And it's in red.

I want to laugh because it means that Amma didn't choose to leave me like one of those babies in the parks.

But I also want to cry because it means Amma is dead.

SUDASA

29

The final
Test is entirely my choice.
No more time to prepare.
Not even for me.

When Asha and I used to play
Tests with our dolls,
she always chose something
        hard
for her final Test.
Something like
What's the square root of 5,950,432?

No matter what the question,
her boy doll would always lose,
whereas mine—
I gave mine
        silly
challenges. Like hopping on one foot
for an hour. Or saying a tongue twister
forty times:

        Sudasa Bala sings songs with her sister by the
            sea.
        Sudasa Bala sings songs with her sister by the
            sea. . . .

As I stare at my two boys—
one with eleven rocks,
the other with thirteen—
I know what I choose,
silly or not,
doesn't matter.

I must act like Nani.
            Ignore the rules.
            Ignore what's fair.
I must keep my promise to Five.
Must make sure my cousin
is the victor.

Of course, this doesn't mean
I must hand him the win
on a brass tray,
so when the director asks me,
"What is your final Test?"
I pause.
Say, "Poetry."

That
will show him how it really feels
to sweat.

Nani repeats my word
as if she hasn't heard it
before.

I say it again, glancing at Papa.
"I want poems.

You know how I love poetry.
I used to read it with my cousin
all the time."

Papa drops his gaze to his book,
and I know his smile is not
for the shahi korma recipe
on his page.

Although Nani opens her mouth,
she closes it before she admits
she's the one
with the pungi.

My cousin seems to forget
his place in the basket.
"That's not a Test," he says,
more to the director
than to me.

When she turns to me, I smile.
"I imagine that will make it
very easy then,
won't it?"

With a raised eyebrow,
the director gives my boys
paper and pencils.

She sends them off.
Off to tell me why they want me.

Or, in one case,
why they don't.

While I wait patiently at the table,
I keep my foot on top of the bag
I stuffed
underneath.

I stare at my parents,
       their elbows only inches from
each other.
       their demeanors
no more intimate
than two high-rise towers.

I imagine
the three of us could really talk.
I'd ask them questions such as
Would you do it again if given the choice?
Would you marry because you had to?
Or would you run—
even if you had nowhere to go,
and no one to go with—
would you run because
staying
meant another kind of death?

My imagination
provides an empty lot
where answers should be.

Even if they could tell me the truth,
it would be like polishing funeral logs.
We can't change the past.
            Not Mummy's.
            Not Papa's.
            Not Nani's.
Not even Koyanagar's.

No, we cannot change
the mistakes we've left behind.
But there's one thing we can do—
one thing I <u>must</u> do—
we can choose not
to repeat them.

CONTESTANT FIVE

30

The rich boy and I are led back to the waiting room. We sit on the perpendicular benches while the middle-aged guard stands by the door. He's there to make sure we don't cheat or fight, although I don't know why—*or how*—we would do either at this point. This last test is a formality. A way to show us that the winner is not chosen by intelligence or by strength or by skill. It's chosen by her.

I take my first piece of paper and write one word: *Goodbye.* I want to say *Good luck,* but that would be admitting that she needs it and I must believe that she does not. She seems smart and she's definitely strong-willed. She'll do just fine without me. Won't she?

I glance across the room. The rich boy looks up from the blank sheets of paper on his lap. He shrugs and grins at the guard. "I've got something to give to that sweet little virgin and it's not a poem."

The guard doesn't smile back. He moves his gaze slowly to meet mine as if he's trying to see if I'll react.

And I do.

In my head.

In my head, I stand up and grab the boy by the front of his kurta. I slam him against the wall and then I drop him to the floor like a sack of manure. I tell him that Sudasa deserves his respect, and not because she's a girl. Because she's a human being. Like him. Like me.

The boy stands, letting his papers and pencil fall to the floor. He continues to address the guard. "I bet you wish it was still the old country, huh? A man should be able to stick it to his wife whenever he wants, and if she doesn't like it, he should be able to slap her senseless. That's the only way they understand who's wearing the pants, right, Mota Bhai?"

This time, the guard's eyes meet mine quickly. He lowers his gaze to the bench. To where I've tightened my fists around my paper, my knuckles turning into snowy peaks. My head is a hurricane of swirling heat. I don't want to drop that disgusting monster on the floor. I want to hold him by the neck until his face goes from red to purple to blue, and when it's almost too late for him to take a final breath, I want to tell him that if he ever talks about Sudasa that way again—if he ever so much as touches one of the silky hairs on her head—I will end him. Then and there.

"Get your papers," the guard says to the rich boy as he whips open the door. "You're going to another room."

The boy exits, flashing me a wink on his way out.

I jump to my feet as the door closes. I kick it with my foot and then I punch it with my fist. I'm about to punch the wall as well when I hear Appa's calm voice in my head.

Patience, boy. Any idiot can fall down. It takes a strong man time to climb up.

Oh, Appa. What I'd give to see you now. You could tell me that it's okay if I deviate from the plan. You could tell me that it's okay to marry Sudasa and make you the brother of your greatest hero. You could tell me that we were both wrong. That Koyanagar is not as bad as we thought.

I sit back down on the bench. No. You could not tell me that and I couldn't believe you if you could. This country is the reason Sudasa and I are both here. It's the reason I don't have my amma and the reason Sudasa might end up the wife of a beast. Everything about Koyanagar is wrong and everything about your plan is right.

I pick up a new piece of paper and scribble *Goodbye* again. I have to leave. Amma or not, it is like *the Mighty Bala* said: the right path to follow, even at the darkest hour. And oh, how dark this hour is. Did Appa know it would be so hard? Would he tell me not to go now that I know Amma is dead? No, of course he wouldn't. Appa wants a better life for me. A life not here. And he cannot know about Amma. He would have told me if he'd found out she was dead. He would have let me mourn her every year on 31 December. He would have mourned her himself.

So why did *the Mighty Bala* leave the registry where I would see it? Did Appa ask him to help me if I needed it? To guide me if I looked lost? Is that what the registry was? A way to give me an extra push in the right direction? Perhaps as far as *the Mighty Bala* is concerned, the fact that Koyanagar caused the deaths of all those boys should be reason enough to leave it. And it is.

I hold my head in my hands. But how can I leave Sudasa in a world like this? And worse, with a boy who will hurt her? It will haunt me for the rest of my days, and I already have enough ghosts.

I lift my head. What if—?

No, it's too risky.

I stand. But I could—?

No, it will never work. Not now that I returned the registry. Unless—?

Could I?

Would I?

Would *she*?

SUDASA

31

The boys return.
    First
my cousin, with his chin leading his strut.
    Last
Five, his gaze low, his brow furrowed.

He seems nervous.
Nervous that I won't keep
my promise.
That I won't set him free.

The director looks my way,
making a sweeping motion
that tells me it's my turn
to perform.

I position myself in front of my cousin.
He holds his paper in his hands.
His shoulders slightly dropped.
His tail between his legs.

I take the paper from him,
my reaction checked
as it unfolds.
I finally have control of the reins.

Too bad the race was won
long ago.

His poem is a forced rhyme
with words like
  fun,
  ton, and
  sun.

They rhyme about our future.
   About the girls we'll have.
   About the girls we'll bring
to Tests like these.

In my head,
I scrunch up his poem.
Throw it in his face.
I tell him that will happen
  over
  my
  dead
  body.
Because I'd rather die
than do
→ THIS ←
to my own child.

With that thought,
the clouds disperse.
My options
turn into

w i d e
blue sky.

All this time
I've been struggling with
who
to choose,
I missed the real point.

The choice I was given
three days ago
was not which
boy
to choose, but which
life.

Like Asha said,
it doesn't matter which boy wins.
The act of accepting the outcome
is a defeat
for everyone.

Was that what Mummy meant
when she said
I must be fair to myself?
Was she saying I must do
what I want?
Not here, in these Tests.
In this life?

Is that what Papa meant

when he said
I would die if I stood still?

Did they both know
my heart would tell me
to do
what they could not?

Did they name me Sudasa
not because they wanted me to obey,
but because they wanted to brand me
with a permanent reminder
of the fact that I exist
because they had?

That Koyanagar exists
because we all do?

That our wall stands
t
a
l
l
because we let it?

The director clears her throat.
I tuck my cousin's words
inside my sari.

For a brief moment,
my hate for him evaporates,

leaving in its place
a **thick** sorrow.

How sad it is that he believes
that winning me
is a victory
>for him.
>for his gender.
>for everyone in Koyanagar.

The director clears her throat again,
so I step over to Five.
I find him back
behind his mask,
and yet his pleading expression is as
naked
as it could be.

I open my palm.
In it he drops a folded square.
I wonder if,
like origami—
>like him?—
it will sprout wings when
I set it free.

I close my fist for a moment.
Pretend I know
what it will say.
>*Please?*
>*You promised?*

Thank you.
Goodbye.

But when I unfold the paper,
I find not a plea.
Not a goodbye.
Nothing but these words:

The fish are at their best
when the sun meets the sea
at the place in Hun Market
where the bananas used to be.
—Kiran

The fish?
Why would he think I want—?
Unless—?
Could he mean Asha? Or girls like Asha?
Like me?
Girls who want a second option?
Who want to escape?
With him?

When the director clears her throat once more,
I remember where I'm
          standing.
Realize what I may be
          holding.

I scrunch my fist.
Freeze

                my breath.
Freeze
                my expression.
Freeze
                my thoughts.

I pretend I'm thinking.
That I need time.
Time
                to consider.
Time
                to slow down.
Time
                to STOP!

I tell time to become a feather
falling
d
  o
    w
      n.
Swaying *s i d e w a y s*
in the warm breeze.

And before I know it,
I'm on the floor.
Voices calling—
calling my name.

32

My head is heavy. Motionless.
I open my eyes.
See a ceiling papered
like a swirling sky.

Swirls of blue looping
in   out
and
in   out
and
the blue
fades to
        gray
            fades to
                  white
                      fades
                          away.

My cheek is cold.
Wet.
I turn to see Mummy
holding a cloth against
my temple.

Her eyes are red—
wet—

and her chin quivers
like jelly.

I turn the other way.
See Papa holding
my hand.
Tight.

As if he's protecting it.
Or protecting what's inside it?
But he can't.
He can't know what ~~Five~~ —
what <u>Kiran</u> wrote.

I start to say, "What happened—"
but Nani cuts me off.

"Nalini," she says, glaring at Mummy,
"this is your fault.
You were supposed to teach
duty,
not
insolence."

The cloth on my face
drops down to my neck,
pressing the ruby drops
HARD
against my throat.

Mummy whips around
and her tiny voice

EXPLODES
like a firecracker
that has been trapped in a crate.

"I'm not the one
who made these Tests,
who decided that children
should have children of their own.
That was you
and your friends in State.
You took your pain
and your anger
and you turned it on her.

"You want us to protect our daughters?
Well, I'm protecting mine.
I'm protecting her from you!"

Mummy points
so Nani will look at me.
At what she has
            done
to me.

But Nani remains
a statue of herself,
her eyes flickering slightly
like a candle
in a breeze.

"You don't understand
what I have been through," Nani says,

stepping into her martyr
costume.
"I chose to keep you
when everyone said to
get rid of you like the others.
Even your father tried to abandon you
in one of those parks,
but I went back for you.
I brought you home.

"He got his revenge
when he up and died and
I had to risk my life—
take charity from my sister—
to put food in your mouth.

"So yes, I fought to change things.
I wanted you to have
the luxuries
I did not:
> *Beautiful clothes.*
> *A penthouse flat.*
> *A husband who could put jewels on your fingers.*

"Still, you do not repay me
with a little respect.
You take those luxuries
and throw them in my face!"

I hear Mummy's breath
turn heavy and loud.

225

"Respect?" she yells.
"Is that what you call
these shackles you've put on me?
You might as well have locked
me in the safe
with your money and
your precious Registry."

Nani's eyes turn to slits,
but Papa speaks calmly
before she lets out her hiss.

"This tug-of-war must end here and now.
Sudasa's not a wishbone
you can break
to get your way."

He turns back to me
and squeezes my hand.
"Beti, are you ready
to put this to an end?"

Something in his eyes
tells me he doesn't mean my ~~Tests~~ tests.
He wants me to be free
of this backward system.

He's not going to help me.
Or tell me what to do.
I must do it because I want to.
Because it's what I̲ choose.

Not
>
> to spite Nani.

Not
>
> to punish my cousin.

Not
>
> to help Asha.

Just to obey <u>me.</u>

I sit up
and say, "I'm ready,"
and I know right then
my heart is, too.

33

The Choosing Ceremony
takes place outside,
on a raised platform
that all can revere
from the surrounding streets.

Rather than using rocks
to award the winners,
each girl gets a jade pendant
that hangs
from a velvet cord.

The jade was chosen
because it symbolizes love.
The round shape
because it symbolizes eternity.

They got one of those right, I suppose.

When it's my turn,
the director calls my name.
She hands me the necklace
and says, *"Please make your choice."*

With the black cord threaded
between my fingers,

I press the cold stone
in my sweaty palm.

I take a step toward Kiran
so I can see how it feels.
It feels right
in a way,
but wrong
just the same.

He made it clear:
he doesn't want to win me.
But his poem—
could it meant that
he doesn't want to lose me, either?

Did it mean that
anyone
could go to the market at sunset
if they were looking for an escape?

Or does
anyone =
me?

I search his eyes
for an answer—
            a confirmation?—
but he darts his hard stare to the right.

And so I veer toward my cousin.

To where he stands,
his teeth a clenched vise.

He believes he has won.
It's clear in his stance.
And I guess he has
won
something.

He might get another chance
        to stand here again.
        to force some
                other boys off the track.
        to intimidate some
                other girl into picking him.

When I place the cord
over his head,
he says, *"It seems your 'Never' has ended."*

Although I force a smile,
to myself I say,
We'll see about that.

I turn to face the crowd,
avoiding Nani's smirk
burning like a spotlight
from the front row.

My cousin reaches out his hand

as if to show we are
one.

I snatch mine away
as if to prove we are
done.

I tuck my hand behind my back,
my fingers wrapped around Kiran's
words.

In my head,
I say these words to my cousin:
You will never touch me.
You will never touch me.
You will
NEVER
NEVER
NEVER
touch me.

A smile crosses my face,
increased by its own irony.
The audience probably
thinks
I'm happy.
And I am.

But not for the reason
they think.

The director dips her thumb
in a silver tub of vermilion.
She brushes a line across
my cousin's forehead
and another across mine.

She hands us each
a plain gold ring. A symbol of
our promise. Our promise
        to show up at the temple.
        to accept the seven blessings.
        to smile when our names are published
on page three of the *Koyanagar News.*

I slip the ring onto the fourth finger
of my right hand.
I remind myself that
promises
in my family
are like the wax seals
we place on our envelopes:
made to be bro   ken.

I look over my shoulder
to see if Kiran
is wondering what I'll do.
If he believes I'll marry my cousin.
If he sees my actions as a response—
        a reaction?
        a rejection?—
to his poem.

I want to find a way
to show him
I'm playing the game.
To let him know
            this is not my real choice.
To let him know
            this is not the end.

But I can't.
It's too late.
The platform is empty.

Kiran is gone.

34

The audience claps.
My heart contracts
as if it's suspended between their hands
as they
>   **POUND.**
>   **POUND.**
>   **POUND.**

I tell myself not to panic.
Kiran had to leave.
Had to go. Go
>   wait for me?

When the audience goes silent,
my cousin joins
his smiling sisters
and Mota Masi,
his grinning nani.

They're off
>   to celebrate.
>   to say goodbye.
>   to send him for the husband training
he won't need to take.

I return inside with the other girls
and their families.
We're supposed to drink champagne
until the losers have dispersed,
but all I want to do
is grab my bag
and join them.

Although I brace myself for a final
snip
from Nani,
she doesn't give me
so much as a glance.

I suppose as far as she's concerned,
her work is done.
I was her pawn and
the game is over.

Of course, if you ask me, I'd say
it has just begun.

She tells Mummy she needs
"to see some friends."
Translation?
She needs to gloat over the women
whose granddaughters
chose the rotten market mangoes.

On her way to follow Nani,
Surina gives me the smug look
I'd been expecting from our matriarch.

She congratulates me
with air-kisses near each of my cheeks.
"Better to play fair for a life of hate,"
she says, twisting my words,
"than cheat for a life of love."

With that, she's gone.
Gone to return to her plastic happiness.
Gone to pretend she's not
crac *king*
at the seams.

I return to our table for my bag.
Say: "I need to use the bathroom."
Know: I need a quick escape.
A quick way
            to say goodbye.
            to rip off the plaster
before I feel the pain.

Papa holds out my bag.
"I suppose you're looking for this,"
he says, hanging it off my shoulder.
Then he places his hand
on my chin and adds,
"Remember, beti,
no bird soars too high,
if he soars with his own wings."

He hugs me tight
and adds in my ear:

"And sometimes, when wings burn,
they rise from the ash
as fins in turn."

He steps back with a smile.
Leaves me wondering
where he got that second quote.
I don't remember it from Blake,
and though he could have made it up,
it would be
an odd coincidence.

He can't know about
Kiran's plan.
He didn't see the poem
and they haven't even met.
Have they?
But when?
Could Papa know Kiran from the market?
Or could Kiran also be from Mannipudi?

Before I can ask,
Papa goes to serve the drinks,
leaving me with Mummy.
She hugs me, too.
   Tight.
   Too tight.
Too tight for her normal self, that is.

"This is a new beginning for you,"

she says as she pulls away,
and wipes the tears from her cheeks.

"Do not let anger over the past
become the fuel that fires your future.
Let it be the love your papa and I
have for you,
because no matter what you do,
that will never, ever go out."

I look into Mummy's glistening eyes.
See
        a girl with a mother
                she could never please.
        a mother with a girl
                she could never not support.

I give her a kiss
        of thanks—
        of goodbye—
then I force myself
to stroll down the hall,
even though
my mind wants to
                sprint!

But it can't because I
must
continue.
Must graciously smile

at the *"Congratulations!"*
shot my way.

Must only wish I had a shield
off which they could bounce.
                    Bounce off me.
→   Hit Nani instead.

When no one is looking,
I duck into the kitchen.
I return to the bathroom
I was in before.

I grab the washbasin.
Steady myself.
Take one last look at
the girl
who won't exist anymore.

No more
        horse-drawn carriages.
        warm dinners.
        feather pillows.

No more
        fancy clothes.
        beaded shoes.
        golden bangles.

No more
        morning rides through the dew.

afternoons reading Blake.
late-night giggles with Asha.

No more
Surina.
Mummy.
Papa.

No more Nani.
No more cousins.

With my breath trapped
inside my chest,
I take out my knife and
hold it to the side
of my neck.

"Time for Act V," I say,
keeping my fists tight.
Then, with a single swipe,
I flick the knife like a crop
and slice off my braid.

I unwind my sari,
and a ring falls to the floor,
the emerald gleam
unmistakable.

Around the gold band is a tiny
piece of paper that says,
For your real *future.*

I know then
Mummy doesn't mean the one with my cousin.
She means the one I can buy
        if I sell her engagement ring.
        if I use the money to find Asha?
Or Kiran?
Or a life that simply isn't here?

I pull the gold band off my right hand.
Replace it with the emerald,
stone facing in.
It will be a secret from the outside world,
and yet a constant reminder to me.

A reminder of how
one thing—
        a ring?
        a decision?
        a law?—
could be both my beginning
and
my end.

I dump out the contents
of my bag. Find Papa's
hat and clothes.
Find something I didn't pack, too.

The Registry?
How did I get the Koyanagar Registry?
It wasn't in the safe.

I know.
I looked for it.

Did Papa put it in here?
No. Nani would never tell him
where she keeps the spare key.
She hasn't even told me.

I bet Mummy knows,
but she didn't bring a bag
to the tests today.
Papa did.
And he was holding my bag
when I came in
from the Choosing Ceremony.

Could Mummy and Papa
have planned this
together?
Could they want me to take
away Nani's most precious
possession? Escape from Koyanagar with
        her secrets?
        her power?
        her sins?

I shove the Registry in my bag,
smothering a bit of a grin.
Nani will be livid
when she finds out it's gone.
Possibly even more livid

than when she finds out
I am, too.

I pull on Papa's hat
and his clothes. Remove
the necklace,
and stuff it in my bag also.

I leave my sari—my suns of luck—
collapsed
in a pile on the floor.
Left to be found when
        clues,
        blame,
        excuses
are sought.

I grab some tissue.
Wipe the powder and vermilion
        from my face.
I rip the bindi
        from my brow.
Unhook the heavy rubies
        from my ears.

I peer into the mirror.
See a
poor
unwanted
boy.

I smile
despite my fear,
because I know
unwanted = free.

I sneak out the door.
Ask the crowd
to let me through.
No one moves
because no one is listening.
Their ears are closed.
My voice is no more.

But invisible as I may be,
I know my actions
scream
LOUDER
than I could
before.

When I make it to the bikes,
there's still quite a stack.
I grab a small gray one
and pretend
it's my horse.

I

        race out of the crowd.
        race down the street.
        race to the future

I choose for me.

Acknowledgments

I must first thank my brilliant editor, Erin Clarke, who is wholly responsible for turning my little Word document into this beautiful book. I must also thank my agent, Lauren MacLeod, whose ability to instantly respond to every single one of my inane questions still astounds me.

I am thankful to Therese Hesketh, Li Lu, and Zhu Wei Xing, whose article in *CMAJ* planted the seeds for this story, but I would not have written it were it not for my friend and personal cheerleader, Jillian Boehme. Every writer needs someone like you, Jill, and I am forever grateful that I have been blessed with your pom-poms in my life.

I owe a huge debt of gratitude to the wonderful Sonali Dev. Everything that is accurate in this book is thanks to you, Sonali, and everything that is not should be blamed on me.

Thank you to my teen readers, Kaitlin Khorashadi and Emily Bertoia.

Special thanks to all of the people who have supported me in this long journey to publication: Yoni Freedhoff, Kimberly

MacCarron, Amy DeLuca, Taryn Albright, Loretta Nyhan, Erica O'Rourke, Christine Nguyen, Mónica Bustamante Wagner, Kerry O'Malley Cerra, Kody Keplinger, Gabrielle Prendergast, Marybeth Smith, Chantal Kirkland, Joanna Volpe, and Sara Kendall. Thank you also to all of the members of the Fearless Fifteeners, Class of 2k15, Lucky 13s, Savvy Seven, and the entire Clan MacLeod. I wish I could name you individually but I'd run out of paper!

Thank you to all of my friends and family, especially those of you who answer my random requests for metaphors on Facebook.

Last but not least, thank you to Simon, Charlotte, and Nicholas. Forever and always, I choose you.

About the Author

Holly Bodger wrote her first book at the age of six. Although the two-page novel about a mouse had a somewhat limited print run of one, the critical acclaim received from her stuffed animals convinced Holly to get an English degree and then, later, to write this book, her debut, which has considerably more than two pages. Holly currently resides in Ottawa, Canada, with her family and a motley crew of both real and stuffed animals.